THIS BOOK BELONGS TO

Name: Haroon Paul

AESOP'S
FABLES

The Donkey's Shadow

AESOP'S FABLES

TIGER BOOKS INTERNATIONAL
LONDON

This edition published in 1993 by
Tiger Books International PLC, Twickenham, England.

© Text and illustrations: Geddes & Grosset Ltd.

ISBN 1 85501 404 1

Printed in Slovenia.

CONTENTS

LIST OF ILLUSTRATIONS

FOX AND GOAT

REYNARD THE FOX left his home one evening and set off for town to see what he could steal for his little ones' supper. In his hurry he fell into a well and couldn't get out. He tried scrambling up the side, but it was no use. Then, just when he was giving up hope and beginning to think he would be drowned, he heard footsteps above. Looking up, he saw the hairy face of Goat peering over the edge of the well.

"Hello," said Goat. "Who are you down there?"

"It's only me—Fox," said Reynard.

"What are you doing down there at this time of night?"

"I was having a drink," answered Fox.

"Is the water good?" asked Goat. "It's been a warm day, and I'm feeling a little thirsty myself."

"Why, the water's delicious!" answered Fox. "I've never tasted such water in my life. Why don't you come and try it? There's plenty left."

Without further talk, Goat jumped into the well. This was just what Fox had been hoping for. Without asking Goat whether he minded, he scrambled up on his back, and with the help of Goat's horns he was able to lift himself to safety.

"Thank you, friend Goat," said Reynard, for he is always polite. "That was most kind of you. Without your help I might never have got out."

Goat looked up at the top of the well and began to call out piteously.

"Oh dear me! I didn't see how deep it was. How am I going to get out?"

"I've no idea," said Reynard. "That's your affair. Didn't your mother ever tell you to look before you leap?"

And with that, Fox turned away and made off towards the town to see what he could steal, leaving poor Goat to get out of the well as best he might.

Look before you leap.

THE MAN AND THE LION

THERE WAS a time when a man and a lion met on the highway, and for some distance journeyed along together quite agreeably. But when the conversation began to concern which creature was superior, a man or a lion, the dispute waxed warmer and warmer.

They were passing a statue which depicted Hercules strangling a lion. "See there!" said the man. "That statue proves that I am right. What stronger proof of man's superiority over a lion could you ask?"

"That doesn't prove a thing," retorted Lion. "Just let us lions be the sculptors and every statue will show a lion standing over a man!"

We are but sorry witnesses in our own cause.

The Fighting Cocks and the Eagles

WO YOUNG cocks were battling fiercely to see which one of them would be the barnyard champion. At last the one that was beaten crept into a corner to hide his wounds and his shame.

But the conqueror flapped his wings and crowed lustily. Then he flew up to the top of the house where he continued to flap his wings and crow so that everyone would be sure to know who was victor. Just then, Eagle, sailing by overhead, spied the crowing Cock. Swooping down he seized him in his talons and carried him off for dinner. Meanwhile the defeated rival came out from his hiding place and took possession of the barnyard over which they had contended.

Pride goeth before a fall.

The Horse and the Stag

 BITTER quarrel arose between the Horse and the Stag in the days when both creatures roamed wild in the forest. Horse came to the hunter to ask him to take his side in the feud.

The hunter agreed, but added: "If I am to help you punish the Stag, you must let me place this iron bit in your mouth and this saddle upon your back."

Horse was agreeable to the man's conditions and he soon was bridled and saddled. The hunter sprang into the saddle, and together they soon had put the Stag to flight. When they returned, Horse said to the hunter: "Now if you will get off my back and remove the bit and the saddle, I won't require your help any longer."

"Not so fast, friend Horse," replied the hunter. "I have you under bit and spur, and from now on you shall remain the slave of man."

Liberty is too high a price to pay for revenge.

Timothy and the Nettles

Timothy was playing in the meadows when he lost his ball. Presently he saw it lying behind a clump of nettles. He put out his hand to take it, and brushing the nettle aside, he was badly stung. He cried with pain and ran in to tell his mother.

"A horrid nettle stung me!" cried Timothy. "I hardly touched it, and now look what it's done!"

He held out his hand, on which the rash was already showing.

"It was because you hardly touched it," said his mother "that it stung you. Next time you meddle with a nettle, grasp it firmly and it won't hurt you. Go and rub your hand with a dock leaf, and remember what I've told you."

What ever you do, do it boldly.

EAGLE AND JACKDAW

THE JACKDAW sat on the branch of a tree, half-way up a steep hill. Below, in the valley, a shepherd was minding his flock. On a crag at the very top of the hill perched a great eagle, King of All Birds. How noble he looked, with his great wings outstretched, ready to swoop, and his eyes fixed on the ground far below!

Then Jackdaw saw Eagle dive down and seize a lamb from the shepherd's flock. He carried it skywards in his mighty talons—and was lost to sight behind the hilltop.

"What a splendid way of catching your dinner!" thought Jackdaw. "Why shouldn't I get mine like that?"

So he too swooped down and fell upon an old ram, whose wool was long and fleecy. But the ram was far too big for him, and he got his feet caught up in the creature's long fleeces. He was so hopelessly entangled that he could not escape. The shepherd came up, and had no difficulty in seizing Jackdaw and keeping him prisoner. He disentangled the bird from the ram's wool and clipped his wings so that he could not fly away. Then the shepherd took Jackdaw home as a pet for his little son.

"Thank you father," said the boy, "but what kind of bird is this?"

"It is a jackdaw," said the shepherd. "He is only a jackdaw—but he thought himself an eagle!"

Pride goes before a fall.

WOLF IN SHEEP'S CLOTHING

To GET HIS living more easily, Wolf thought of a plan: "If I can manage to live along with those sheep," he said to himself, "I can run off with one of them when I get a chance. But if I go like this, the shepherd will notice me and set his dogs on me and drive me off. He might even get a gun and shoot me."

So he took the skin of a sheep that had died up in the hills, and dressed himself carefully in it, making sure to cover up all his own grey hair. Then he slipped in among the sheep, and wasn't noticed. At night he was shut in the pen, along with the flock.

"When all's quiet," he thought, with a cunning smile, "I'll kill one of these fat sheep and have a better meal than I ever had in my life."

But the shepherd, before going home, remembered that he had meant to kill a sheep for his own dinner next day. So he took a sharp knife and went back into the pen. But the sheep that he killed in the dark was not a sheep at all—it was Wolf, dressed up in sheep's clothing.

Laziness may be our ruin.

The Wolf in Sheep's Clothing

The Ant and the Grasshopper

DONKEY IN LION'S SKIN

INDING THE skin of a lion that had died, Donkey put it on and wore it as if it were his own. He covered up his dusty grey hair with the lion's tawny hide.

"What a splendid overcoat!" said Donkey to himself. "Now I'm just like Lion, King of All Animals."

So he went prancing about the countryside, frightening all the timid creatures he could find. First he saw Rabbit and galloped up to him, roaring as loudly as he could. Rabbit scuttled away into his burrow.

Then Donkey came upon Goat and frightened him in the same way, till Goat ran up a steep hillside as fast as he could run.

Donkey felt very pleased with himself, and laughed aloud to think how he was playing at being King of the Beasts.

"Why," he thought, "I only have to put on Lion's skin to be as fierce and terrible as Lion himself. Here comes Fox! Let's see if I can scare him."

So as soon as Reynard was near, Donkey crouched as low as he could and tried to look as savage and terrible as Lion.

He growled ferociously, but to Reynard it sounded just like "Ee-aw! Ee-aw!"

So Reynard only laughed and ran right up to Donkey; he lifted the corner of Lion's skin and saw Donkey's dusty grey hair.

"Good day, Your Majesty," said Reynard slyly. "I shouldn't be surprised to see a pair of long ears under that mane of yours. Why, what a donkey you are, to think you could frighten me! Whoever heard a lion bray like that?''

And he ran off to tell all the other animals what a donkey Donkey was, and how silly they had been to be scared of him.

If you play a part you are not fitted for,
you're sure to give yourself away.

ANT AND GRASSHOPPER

ALL SUMMER THE ant had been working hard, gathering a store of corn for the winter. Grain by grain she had taken it from the fields and stowed it away in a hole in the bank, under a hawthorn bush.

One bright, frosty day in winter Grasshopper saw her. She was dragging out a grain of corn to dry it in the sun. The wind was keen, and poor Grasshopper was cold.

"Good morning, Ant," said he. "What a terrible winter it is! I'm half dead with hunger. Please give me just one of your corn grains to eat. I can find nothing, although I've hopped all over the farmyard. There isn't a seed to be found. Spare me a grain, I beg."

"Why haven't you saved anything up?" asked Ant. "I worked hard all through the summer, storing food for the winter. Very glad I am too, for as you say, it's bitterly cold."

"I wasn't idle last summer, either," said Grasshopper.

"And what did you do, pray?"

"Why, I spent the time singing," answered Grasshopper. "Every day from dawn till sunset I jumped about or sat in the sun, chirruping to my heart's content."

"Oh you did, did you?" replied Ant. "Well, since you've sung all summer to keep yourself cheerful, you may dance all winter to keep yourself warm. Not a grain will I give you!"

And she scuttled off into her hole in the bank, while Grasshopper was left cold and hungry.

In good times prepare for when the bad times come.

THE STAG AT THE POOL

STAG WENT down to a pool to drink. As he lapped the cool water, he noticed his reflection, and said to himself: "What magnificent antlers I have! How slender and graceful they are, and how delicately curved and branched. But it's a pity about my skinny legs and small feet. They rather spoil my good looks."

At that moment a hunting horn was heard, and a pack of hounds streamed down the hill towards the pool, followed by two or three huntsmen on horseback.

Instantly Stag stopped drinking and took to his heels. He coursed over the fields until he came to the shelter of a thicket. His legs had carried him beyond the reach of the hounds, but his antlers got caught in the branches of a tree. He only just managed to free himself before the hounds came in sight, and once more he ran for his life. When he had thrown off the pursuit, he stood still, panting and breathless.

"Ah," said Stag, "I shouldn't have spoken badly of the legs and feet that nature gave me. They saved my life. As for my beautiful antlers, they were almost my undoing."

Use is of more importance than ornament.

MICE AND WEASELS

HE MICE were having a war with the Weasels. But Weasels are bigger and fiercer and are more than a match for Mice. So the Mice had a meeting to decide what to do.

"Let's chose leaders," one of them said. "We shall never beat the Weasels if each of us fights for himself, and there is no one to give orders. Let us have generals, to give orders and plan the battle."

Immediately the biggest and strongest Mice pushed themselves forward and said they would be the generals. The others agreed, and once more they went out to battle.

Now the generals, in order to make themselves look bigger and more important than the other Mice, tied horns on their heads. Then everyone would know they were the leaders.

When the Weasels came, the Mice were ready for them. They fought bravely for an hour or more, but many of the Mice were killed, and the generals decided they must retreat. So they gave the order, and all the Mice scuttled back into their holes, which were too small for the Weasels to follow them. But the generals got their tall horns caught, and could not get back into the holes fast enough. So they were set on by the Weasels and quickly destroyed.

After that, no more Mice came forward and offered to be leaders.

There is danger in being a leader.

THE GOD MERCURY

THE ROMANS had many gods. The chief of them all was Jupiter, and his wife was Juno. Their messenger, who used to travel between heaven and earth, was the swift-winged Mercury. One day Mercury thought he would like to know what the people on earth thought about him. Did they think him a great god, he wondered, or did they rate him at little value? Overcome with curiosity, he paid a visit to the earth.

In a certain city there was a sculptor named Lucius, who made clay images of the gods. These he sold to the people to set up in their houses. When Mercury came down to earth, he disguised himself as a traveller and went into Lucius' shop.

"Good day, friend," he said. "Have you some figures of the chief gods for sale?"

"I have indeed, sir," answered the sculptor, stopping his work to wipe his hands on his apron. "What god are you interested in?"

"How much do you want for this figure of Jupiter?" asked Mercury, picking up a small clay model of the ruler of the gods.

"Well, I could let you have that for a silver piece," answered Lucius.

"I see," said Mercury, laughing to himself.

"So that's what the All-High God is worth—one silver piece," he thought. "That's not much."

But he only said:

"And this one of Juno, the goddess of women—how much does

that cost?"

"That's a bit more," answered Lucius. "I'd have to ask two silver pieces for Juno."

"Really?" said Mercury. "Now what about this—how much would you ask for this handsome figure?"

And he picked up a small statue of himself, the god Mercury.

"Oh that," answered the sculptor. This time it was his turn to laugh. "I can't very well ask much for him—let's see… I tell you what. If you give me the price I ask for the other two, I'll throw in Mercury for nothing!"

Mercury was so angry that he stamped out of the shop without another word.

If you try to find out what other people think of you,
you may be disappointed.

LEOPARD AND FOX

THE LEOPARD WAS putting the finishing touches to his toilet. He lay in the sun, admiring the beauty of his sleek, smooth coat, so elegantly marked. He rose lazily and strolled over to the pool, the better to gaze at himself in the clear water.

"R-r-r-really," he purred, "I am indeed beautiful. Of all the animals in the forest, I am certainly the finest."

"I don't know so much about that," said Fox, who was passing at the time and happened to overhear him. Leopard pretended not to hear.

"It's those spots," went on Reynard more loudly. "What a pity you can't change them!"

Leopard looked down his nose at Fox in a lordly way.

"And who are you to talk?" he said at last, showing his sharp white teeth and curling his tail scornfully. "With that scrubby ginger coat of yours and that bedraggled brush, I wonder you dare show yourself in public."

"I think I heard you say you were the finest creature in the forest," said Reynard. "How do you make that out?"

"*You* may not like my spots," answered Leopard, "but most creatures admire them greatly. Then I have such sleek, luxuriant fur, such a graceful shape, and such a noble way of moving. But I suppose you think yourself even finer."

"Indeed I do," answered Reynard. "I may not have your spots and your glossy finish. I may not be able to creep about like a snake. But I have brains, my dear chap. I'm the cleverest, craftiest, cunningest animal in the whole creation. Why, everyone envies me my intelligence! As for you, you've no more wit than a hen that's why I'm finer than you!"

And without waiting for an answer he sped off into the woods after a rabbit.

Good looks aren't everything.

THE HEDGE AND THE VINEYARD

FOOLISH young heir came into the possession of his wise father's estate. After the funeral and when his inheritance was securely in his hands, the young man ordered his servants to cut down all of the hedges that surrounded his vineyard. When the servants sought to dissuade their new master from his purpose he shouted: "Why should they not be torn down? They bear no grapes; they yield no harvest; they occupy good land that should be planted to vines.Pull them up and burn them."

So the fences were torn down and the vineyard was open to the ravages of man and beast, and it was not long before the vines were all destroyed. And thus the simple fellow learned, when it was too late, that while it is true that one ought not to expect to gather grapes from brambles, yet it is quite as important to protect one's vineyard as to possess it.

They also serve who only stand and wait.

WAR-HORSE AND DONKEY

TOILING ALONG the road, Donkey bore a heavy load of stones for repairing the farmyard wall. It was a hot day, and poor Donkey was almost worn out. Presently he heard the thunder of hooves. A splendid war-horse was approaching along the road, his harness jingling and his saddle-cloth flapping gaily as he galloped along.

"Out of my way, Ass!" called the war-horse. "I am the proud Tarquin, and I am off to the wars."

Donkey said nothing, but obediently stumbled to the side of the road, just in time to let Tarquin pass.

"Be more careful, you dolt!" shouted Tarquin over his shoulder. "I nearly trampled you under my hooves."

Donkey plodded patiently on up the dusty road, while the horse galloped off to the war.

Not long afterwards there was a battle, and Tarquin was wounded. An arrow struck him in the shoulder and he was so badly hurt that he was no longer fit to be a war-horse. He was put to work on the farm.

One day Donkey saw him struggling into the yard drawing a huge cart. He was panting wearily, and called to Donkey for help.

"Give us a hand with this wagon," he said. "I'm not used to this sort of work, and it's killing me."

"No," said Donkey. "You should have thought of that when you nearly trampled on me in the road. I'm having my rest now, and it's no use asking me for help."

The proud cannot look for help to those they have slighted.

TOWN MOUSE AND COUNTRY MOUSE

THE COUNTRY Mouse lived in a cornfield deep in the countryside. Her life was calm and unexciting. One day a mouse from the town came that way, and Country Mouse invited her to dinner. They sat down in the fields and had a picnic of barley grains.

Town Mouse didn't think much of it.

"Is this how you live all the year round?" she asked, twirling her whiskers. "Not much to do here, is there?"

"I live well enough," answered Country Mouse. "When the weather's fine, I play in the fields. When it's wet, I take shelter in a barn. Nobody bothers me, and I don't have to trouble about looking smart or entertaining fine visitors."

"But is this all you have to eat?" asked Town Mouse in a very haughty voice.

"It's plain," said Country Mouse, "but it's wholesome; and there's plenty of it. I never go short of a meal, and I never have a day's illness. You should come and stay with me some time."

"I should die of boredom," said Town Mouse, hiding a yawn behind her well-groomed paw. "But you'd better visit me. Then you'll see what life can be like."

So next day Country Mouse went to dinner with Town Mouse.

"What a fine place you have, to be sure!" she said, admiring the great house and the pretty garden, full of flowers and vegetables of all sorts.

Town Mouse lived in a larder, which was always stored with meats and cheeses of every description.

"Yes, indeed," said Town Mouse. "This is something like life! Why, there's never a dull moment! Come on, let's have dinner. Now, what will you take? I can give you a little roast chicken—or will you begin with cheese and biscuits? I have a particularly fine gorgonzola this week."

"Well, that's very kind of you," said Country Mouse. "Now which shall it be? I rather think—"

But just at that moment the door of the larder was pushed open, and a pair of heavy boots walked in.

"Look out," said Town Mouse. "We'd better hide behind this bread bin for a minute or two."

The two mice went into hiding. Country Mouse could see that Town Mouse was trembling with fear.

"As you say," she said when the boots had gone, "never a dull moment. Well, suppose I try a little cheese?"

No sooner had she got her teeth into the gorgonzola than the boots came back. Nasty, big, ugly things they were too! Once more the mice scuttled behind the bread bin till the intruder had gone. This time the door was left open, so the poor mice stayed behind the bin, nibbling their dinner and scarcely daring to speak. All at once there was a sound of paws, and a grey cat snuffed her way into the larder. Town Mouse dropped what she was eating and took flight down a hole in the floor. Country Mouse followed her, but she didn't wait any longer. Instead, she told Town Mouse that this sort of life would be the death of her, and ran off back to the country as fast as she could go.

She sat down in her own cornfield and began eating a barley grain.

"This is the life for me," she said to herself. "Let Town Mouse keep her fine house and her splendid food. It would never suit me. What's the good of all the meat and cheese in the world if you can never sit down and enjoy it in peace?"

A plain life and a safe one is better
than fine fare without security.

MONKEY AND FISHERMAN

THE MONKEY sat in a palm tree overlooking the river. Presently two fishermen came along. They carried a net between them, which they stretched from bank to bank, so that it hung down in the water. In this way they would catch the fish that swam up or down the stream. Then the two men went away to eat their dinner and wait.

"That's a good idea," thought Monkey, and as soon as the fishermen were out of sight, he jumped down from the tree. He ran to a spot where he knew there was an old fishing net; and this he dragged down to the water and tried to do the same as he had seen the men do. But he had never tried fishing before, and very soon he got so tangled up in the net that he nearly drowned. He choked and spluttered in the water, and it was only with the greatest difficulty that he managed to tear himself free and get safely to shore.

"That's the last time I go fishing," he said to himself. "In future I'd better stick to coconuts."

Don't meddle with what you don't understand.

Oak and Reed

A GREAT OAK tree stood on a hill, and a slender reed grew at its foot. When the wind blew, the reed swayed and shook, but the oak remained firm.

The tree looked down at the little reed and called to him:

"Why do you tremble so when the wind blows? Why don't you keep still, like me?"

"I'm not as strong as you," said the reed in his small piping voice. "I could never stand up in a wind."

"Then you must be a coward," said the oak scornfully, "and a poor sort of plant. You should learn to stand up for yourself. Just take a lesson from me."

And the oak stood on the hill, taller and stronger than ever.

But soon there came a great storm. A mighty wind blew from off the sea and made a terrible roaring, so that people said they had never heard a gale like this one in all their lives. The oak stood firm and the slender reed bowed before the wind until it touched the ground. All night long the wind blew, and when in the morning it ceased, the reed stood up again, but the oak lay flat on the ground, smashed down by the force of the gale.

The proud will be destroyed, but the humble will outlive
their misfortunes.

LION AND FOX

HE KING Lion one day sent to Fox to come and speak with him. Reynard obeyed. Bowing deeply before the king, he said: "What can I do for Your Majesty?"

Lion looked down his royal nose at the sly little creature before him.

"Fox," he said graciously, "you are a crafty and resourceful animal."

Reynard bowed his head, and wondered what was coming next.

"My eyesight is not what it was," Lion went on. "When I go hunting, I don't see my prey as easily as I used to. I am a fierce and deadly hunter, but I have need of a servant to find my prey and point him out to me. Will you do this? I will see that you have a share in whatever I kill. I, of course, will have the lion's share, but you shall not go hungry."

Reynard gladly accepted this honourable position, and became King Lion's servant.

For a time all went well. Fox would lead Lion through the thickets and among the rocks, and whenever his sharp little eyes caught sight of a goat or a deer, he would signal noiselessly to his master. Lion would instantly bound towards the helpless creature and kill it. And he always gave Reynard a share.

But one day Reynard said to himself:

"This is all very fine. Hunting is now an easy matter for the king, since he has my sharp eyes and keen nose to depend on. He may be brawny, but I am the brains of the partnership. Why should he have all the fun of the kill? Besides, everyone says what a mighty hunter he is. Nobody thinks of me."

So he said to Lion:

"Your Majesty, now that I have seen you hunt, I think I know something about it. I would like to do the killing myself. Will you allow me to have a try?"

"By all means, my dear fellow," said Lion. "Just you go ahead."

Fox, very pleased with himself, soon spied out a herd of deer, and without waiting for Lion to follow him, he sped towards them. At that instant a huntsman on a swift horse rode up in pursuit of the herd. Catching sight of Fox, he reined in his horse and lifted his gun to his shoulder. A bullet whistled past Reynard's ear, and at the sound of the gun he nearly died of fright. He gave up chasing the herd and returned to King Lion, looking very sorry for himself. After that, he left the killing to his master and contented himself with pointing out the prey.

Do the work you are suited for,
and don't attempt what is beyond you.

The Old Woman and the Physician

An old woman, who had become blind, called for a physician to attend her.

"Since you are a healer of such great renown," she said, "I would like to strike a bargain with you. If you will restore my eyesight I will give you a most handsome reward. But if, within a reasonable time, you fail and my malady still remains, then you shall receive nothing."

The physician, observing that the old woman was comfortably off and had many possessions, concluded the agreement. So he called regularly and pretended to treat the woman's eyes, meanwhile, bit by bit, carrying off all her goods.

After a time, whatever had been causing the old lady's blindness disappeared, and she found her sight again. Thereupon the physician demanded the stipulated fee. But discovering that nearly all of her possessions had disappeared since the coming of the physician, she kept putting him off with excuses. At length he grew impatient and had his patient summoned before a judge.

When called upon for her defense, the old woman said: "What this man says is true enough. I promised to give him his fee if my sight were restored, but nothing if my eyes remained blind. Now then, he says that I am cured, but it cannot be true. For before my malady came upon me I could see all sorts of furniture and goods in my house. But now I cannot see a single stick, yet he tells me that he has restored my sight!"

He who plays a trick must be prepared to take a joke.

Birdcatcher and Partridge

S O CATCH BIRDS in search of food, Peter the birdcatcher used to go out with his nets and lay them cunningly among the bushes. Then he would kill them and sell them in the market. One day he caught a fat partridge. The bird cried out piteously and spoke to Peter.

"Oh Mr. Birdcatcher, I beg you to let me go. I never did you any harm. Oh, spare my life, I beg you!"

"I don't know so much about that," said Peter. "Why should I let you go, eh?"

"If you will spare my life," answered the partridge, "I might be useful to you. I can sit beside your net and attract other birds into it. As you know, birds of a feather flock together; and many a young partridge will I lead into your snare."

"Why, you miserable traitor!" cried Peter scornfully. "I might have let you go, but now I shall do no such thing. No creature deserves to live who is cowardly enough to save his own skin by betraying his friends."

Only a coward betrays his fellows.

THE MILLER, THE BOY AND THE DONKEY

THE MILLER, Old John, was a good-natured man, and always tried to please everyone.

"We don't need that donkey any more," said his wife. "You can get a good price for him now, John, if you take him into town next market day."

So Old John set off with his young son Jack, and led the donkey along the road to the town.

Presently a party of girls passed them, and when they saw the miller and his donkey, they laughed.

"Fancy walking to town on a hot day like this," one of them said, "when you've got a donkey to carry you!"

Old John hadn't thought of this.

"Why of course," he said. "Up you get, my boy, and let him save you a walk."

He helped Jack on to the donkey's back, and off they went once more.

Soon they passed a company of old men sitting outside an inn.

"Well, I declare!" said one old man. "Do you see that? Look at that young lad riding the donkey, while the old man has to walk alongside!"

"Ay," said another, "just what I was saying. Young folks are all selfish nowadays, and never think of their elders. Hi, young 'un, let the old man have a turn on the donkey!"

"Perhaps they're right," said the miller. "Would you mind getting down now, Jack, and letting your old father have a ride?"

So Jack and his father changed places, and jogged on towards the town. Very soon they caught up with a party of women, and one of them said:

"Now, isn't that too bad! Just look at the selfish old man, riding on the donkey, while the little lad runs along behind! The poor little chap can hardly keep up with him. It's downright cruel, that it is, on a day like this."

"Well, perhaps you'd better come up behind me," said Old John to his son. "I think there's room for both."

So with both of them astride the donkey, they reached the outskirts of the town. Here they were met by a townsman, out for a walk with his dog. He looked at them and said:

"How can you have the heart to overload that poor beast on a day like this? You're just as well able to carry that old donkey between you, you two, as he is to carry you!"

"Just as you say," said Old John, anxious to please the townsman. And indeed, the donkey was somewhat the worse for wear. So he and Jack got down from his back and tied his four legs together. They took a strong pole, thrust it between the donkey's legs, and hoisted him on to their shoulders. Then, with the donkey swinging upside down between them, the miller and his son made their way into the town.

Well, they looked so ridiculous that all the people came out to see them. How they laughed and cheered to see such a strange sight! Just as they reached a bridge over the river that runs beside the town, the donkey was alarmed by the cheering and shouting, as well as by his extreme discomfort. So he kicked with all his might and broke loose from the pole. But he couldn't stop himself from plunging over the side of the bridge, and falling with a great splash into the water.

"That's what comes of trying to suit everyone," said the old man in disgust. "Come on, my boy, let's be getting home."

Old John the Miller had lost his donkey, and there was nothing for it but to turn round and go back the way he had come.

It's no use trying to please everyone.

WIDOW MARTIN AND HER HEN

THERE WAS ONCE A widow called Old Jenny Martin who lived by herself. She had one fine hen which laid her an egg a day, a beautiful fresh egg with a smooth brown shell. Not content with this, she said to herself:

"Every day I give that hen two handfuls of barley, and she lays me one egg. Now if I was to give her four handfuls, perhaps she'd lay me two eggs."

So she went to the bin and took out four handfuls of barley, and the hen pecked it all up in no time.

Next morning the widow went hopefully to the henhouse, but there was still only one egg. The day after, it was the same. Widow Martin gave the hen four handfuls, but she only got one egg in exchange. Worse than that, the extra food soon made the hen so fat and lazy that she stopped laying altogether. So poor Widow Martin had no eggs at all.

Figures don't always work out as we want them to.

Birds, Beasts and Bats

MANY YEARS ago there was a war between the birds and the beasts. Eagle and Hawk swooped down and carried off little creatures like Mole and Rabbit; and to get their revenge, Serpent and Cat stole the birds' eggs from their nests and killed the birds whenever they could catch them. Every creature in the world took sides—except one, Bat.

"I will see which is strongest," said Bat to himself, "and take whichever side looks like winning."

With his great leathery wings he could easily pass for a bird, and with his ears and claws he could equally well be taken for a beast.

When the beasts were doing well, and looked like killing all the birds, Bat said he was a beast and fought against the birds. But when the birds were doing well, he flew round like a bird and killed little mice in the fields and hedges. It was a fierce war and went on for many months.

At last both beasts and birds grew tired of fighting and made peace. Both sides promised never to start another war, though I am sorry to say they have not always kept their word. But because of the way he had behaved during the fighting, neither side would have Bat.

"You fought for the beasts!" cried the Eagle, King of Birds. "You may go and be a beast."

"You were on the side of the birds," said the Lion, King of All Animals, "so of course you must be a bird!"

So from that day to this, Bat has never really been sure whether he is beast or bird, and has skulked about by night and made his home in the roof of barns. He flies like a bird, but does not sit in the trees by day and sing. So nobody knows exactly what kind of creature he is.

Nobody likes a turncoat.

THE LION AND THE BULLS

HE LION often prowled about a pasture where three bulls grazed together. He had tried without success to lure one or the other of them to the edge of the pasture. He had even attempted a direct attack, only to see them form a ring so that from whatever direction he approached he was met by the horns of one of them.

Then a plan began to form in Lion's mind. Secretly he started spreading evil and slanderous reports of one bull against the other. The three bulls, distrustingly, began to avoid one another, and each withdrew to a different part of the pasture to graze. of course, this was exactly what Lion wanted. One by one he fell upon the bulls, and so made easy prey of them all.

United we stand; divided we fall.

"Wolf! Wolf!"

Shepherd boy Paul lived in a village not far from a great forest. Every day he went out to the fields to mind his master's sheep. Now there were wolves in that forest, and Paul thought he would play a joke on the people of his village. One day he shouted out at the top of his voice, in a tone of great alarm:

"Wolf! Wolf!—Come quickly—the wolf is after my sheep!"

Some of the villagers came rushing out with sticks and stones to drive away the enemy. But when they reached Paul, he was laughing at them.

"How funny you all look," he said, "charging through the fields with your sticks and stones to frighten away a wolf that isn't here! Oh dear, I shall never stop laughing."

Angrily the villagers went back home. They didn't think Paul's joke was at all funny.

A week or so later he played the same trick. The villagers thought he must really be in trouble this time. Once more they ran to his help, and once more they found the sheep safe and sound, with not a wolf in sight.

"The boy's a liar," one of the villagers said. "He won't get me out again with his lying tales!"

Then a few days later a wolf did come out of the forest, and ran straight towards one of Paul's sheep.

"Wolf! Wolf!" cried Paul, terrified. "Help me, good neighbours, I pray. Help, help!"

But this time the villagers who heard him said to each other:

"There's that wicked boy up to his tricks again! But he won't make a fool of us this time."

And they took no notice and went on with their work.

With no one to help him, Paul could not drive away the wolf, which pounced upon the sheep and ran off with it into the forest. So Paul's thoughtless joke had cost his master one of his flock.

Liars are not believed even when they tell the truth.

VENUS AND THE CAT

MANY YEARS ago there was a cat who fell in love with a handsome young man. She prayed and prayed to Venus, the Goddess of Love, to give her the young man for a husband. So Venus, taking pity on the cat, changed her into a beautiful young lady. The man saw her and instantly fell in love. So the two were married, and the man took home the young lady as his bride.

But had she really changed, or was she still a cat underneath? Venus wanted to find out.

One day the goddess sent a little mouse into the lady's house, where she was sitting with her husband. At first the young lady did not notice the mouse, but suddenly she saw it. She made a quick movement and sprang upon it, and almost before the young man had seen the mouse, it was dead.

"So," said Venus to herself, "she may look like a young lady, but she behaves like a cat."

And the goddess was so angry that she changed the young lady back into a cat, and the young man never saw her again.

We cannot change our true nature.

The Old Lady and her Maids

HERE WAS once an old lady who kept two maids called Sally and Sue. She worked them very hard, for she was a mean old lady and liked to get all she could for her money. But Sally and Sue didn't mind hard work: what they minded was having to get up the moment the cock crew. For that is what the old lady made them do. Every morning, whether it was at five o'clock or four, as soon as the cock crew in the yard, the old lady called to Sally and Sue to bestir themselves and begin the day's work.

"This won't do at all," said Sally. "I hate that old cock, I do."

"So do I," said Sue. "If only he'd forget to crow, we might get a bit of sleep for once."

"I tell you what," said Sally, "let's get rid of him. Then he can't crow any more."

So they went to the yard when the old lady was out visiting one day, and wrung the cock's neck, so that he would never more wake them up in the morning.

But now the old lady missed the sound of "Cock-a doodle-do" in the morning, and she was so worried for fear the maids would oversleep, that she took to calling them herself. She wasn't content with four or five o'clock—she sometimes woke at midnight and made the girls get up earlier than ever. So Sally and Sue did themselves no good by killing the cock.

It doesn't pay to be too clever.

JUPITER AND THE BEE

MANY YEARS ago there was an industrious bee who had stored her combs with a bountiful harvest. One day she decided to fly up to heaven to present an offering of honey to Jupiter. The god was so delighted with the bee's girth that he promised her she should have whatever her heart desired.

"Oh, great Jupiter, my creator and my master, I beg of thee, give thy servant a sting, so that when anyone approaches my hive to take the honey, I may kill him on the spot."

Jupiter was surprised to hear such a bloodthirsty request from such a humble creature. Becoming angry, he said: "Your prayer shall not be granted in exactly the way you wish. But the sting you ask for you shall have. When anyone comes to take away your honey and you attack him, the wound shall be fatal. But it shall be fatal to you, for your life shall go with your sting."

He who prays hard against his neighbour
brings a curse upon himself.

FOX AND CROW

ITTING ON THE branch of a tree, Crow had a piece of cheese in his beak. He had just stolen it from a farm kitchen, where he had seen it through the open window. Reynard the Fox looked up and saw Crow on the branch, and he thought how much he would enjoy that fine fresh piece of cheese.

"Good day, Crow," said Reynard. But Crow said nothing. He had the cheese in his beak.

"You know," Reynard went on, "I've never really noticed what a beautiful bird you are."

Crow bent down slightly in order to hear better.

"The smoothness and blackness of your coat is so handsome, so dignified. Your feathers are much lovelier—to my mind—than Peacock's. His are so gaudy, don't you think?"

Still Crow said nothing. But he was most interested.

"Then your neck," Reynard continued, "why, it is as proud and noble as Eagle's, and everyone knows thathe is King of Birds. As for your eye—not even Hawk has a brighter and more resplendent eye! Yes indeed, but for one thing, I would say you are worthy to be King of all the birds."

Crow was preening himself and grooming himself with pride. He had never been so flattered in all his life.

"Yes," sighed Fox, "what a pity it is that with all your beauty you should have no voice! If only you knew how to sing."

This was too much for poor Crow. Perhaps he hadn't a voice

like Nightingale's, but at least he could "caw" in a way which some listeners might not think too bad. He would show Reynard! So taking a deep breath and closing his eyes, he opened his beak and gave out a loud "Caw, caw!"

Of course the cheese instantly fell out of his mouth, and Reynard caught it and gobbled it up.

Never listen to flattery.

The Lion and his Three Counsellors

THE KING OF Beasts was in an irritable mood. That morning his mate had told him that his breath was most unpleasant. After doing considerable roaring to prove that he was king he summoned his counsellors.

First he called Sheep.

"Friend Sheep," he roared, opening wide his great mouth, "would you say that my breath smells unpleasant?"

Believing that Lion wanted an honest answer, Sheep gave it, and the King of Beasts bit off her head for a fool.

Then he called Wolf and asked him the same question. Wolf, catching sight of the carcass of the sheep, said: "Why, your majesty, you have a breath as sweet as blossoms in the spring—"

Before he could finish he had been torn to pieces for being a flatterer.

At last Lion called Fox and put the question to him. Fox gave a hollow cough, then cleared his throat. "Your majesty," he whispered, "truly, I have such a cold in the head that I cannot smell at all."

In dangerous times wise men say nothing.

THE CAT AND THE FOX

Fox was boasting to Cat one day about how clever he was. "Why, I have a whole bag of tricks," he bragged. "For instance, I know of at least a hundred different ways of escaping my enemies, the dogs."

"How remarkable," said Cat. "As for me, I have only one trick, though I usually make it work. I wish you could teach me some of yours."

"Well, sometime when I have nothing else to do," said Fox, "I might teach you one or two of my easier ones."

Just at that moment they heard the yelping of a pack of hounds. They were coming straight toward the spot where Cat and Fox stood. Like a flash Cat scampered up a tree and disappeared in the foliage. "This is the trick I told you about," she called down to Fox. "It's my only one. Which trick are you going to use?"

Fox sat there trying to decide which of his many tricks he was going to employ. Nearer and nearer came the hounds. When it was quite too late, Fox decided to run for it. But even before he started, the dogs were upon him, and that was the end of Fox, bagful of tricks and all!

One good plan that works is better
than a hundred doubtful ones.

HERCULES AND THE WAGONER

THE LAZY FARM hand was carelessly driving his wagon along a muddy road, when the wheels became stuck so fast in the clay that the horses could no longer pull the load.

The wagoner got down, and without making the least effort toward extricating the cart from the mire, he began to pray for Hercules, the God of Strength, to come and help him out of his trouble.

But Hercules, annoyed by the man's helplessness, called down from above: "Get up from your knees, lazybones, and put your shoulder to the wheel."

The gods help them that help themselves.

THE LIONESS

 IVALRY EXISTED among the beasts of the forest over which could produce the largest litter. Some shamefacedly admitted having only two, while others boasted proudly of having a dozen.

At last the committee called upon the Lioness.

"And to how many cubs do you give birth?" they asked the proud Lioness.

"One," she replied sternly, "but that one is a lion!"

Quality is more important than quantity.

LION, GOAT AND VULTURE

THE DAY WAS very hot. Lion and Goat were both thirsty, but the pool was small. Goat bent down his head to drink, when Lion came up beside him and growled fiercely.

"I shall drink first," he said. "I am King of All the Animals, and it is my right. Get out of my way!"

"No," said Goat, "I shall drink first. I found the water. You can wait till I've finished."

"You'll drink it all up," said Lion. "There's not very much left, and I am nearly dead with thirst."

"And I haven't had a drop all day," answered Goat.

So they quarrelled. Lion chased Goat to the top of a great rock, and, hot as he was, Goat bounded out of the way. Neither of them was able to drink in peace.

Suddenly Lion stopped chasing Goat and looked up into the hot blue sky. Goat looked too. There, circling slowly above them, was Vulture. All the animals knew and feared him. He is the Bird of Death, who waits to pounce on the bodies of dead animals and eat their flesh. Lion and Goat knew, both at once, that if they did not stop fighting, they would die of thirst, and Vulture would pick their bodies to the bone.

"If we go on quarrelling," said Lion, "we shall both die of thirst, and that will be the end of us. Go to the water and drink, but don't take it all!"

Goat did as he was told, and the two animals quenched their thirst instead of fighting.

When a common danger threatens, it is best to stop quarrelling.

BOAR AND FOX

THE FOX WAS walking in the woods one day when he heard a rasping sound.

"I wonder what that can be," he said to himself, and went on cautiously.

Presently he came to a clearing, and there, sharpening his tusks on a tree trunk, stood a wild boar. How keen and white his two pointed tusks looked! Reynard stood and watched.

"Now tell me why you're doing that," he said at length.

"I have to keep my tusks sharp," said Boar, pausing in his work. "They're my only weapons, you know. I'm not a swift runner like you, and I haven't got claws like a tiger. So when I fight, I have to use my teeth."

"But there isn't a huntsman or a hound in sight," answered Reynard. "You've nothing to fear."

"Perhaps not," was the reply, "but when the hunters and the dogs do come after me, it'll be too late to sharpen my weapons then."

And Wild Boar took no further notice of Fox, but went on pointing his tusks against the tree.

When the enemy is upon you,
it is too late to make ready your weapons.

TOM IN THE RIVER

OM SPLASHED lazily about in the river. The day was warm. There was no wind, and the sun shone down out of a clear blue sky. He was only a little boy and had not yet learnt to swim properly, so of course he shouldn't have gone into the middle of the water, out of his depth. Suddenly he discovered that he couldn't touch the bottom.

Tom tried to struggle to safety; then he saw a stranger coming towards him.

"Help!" he shouted as loudly as he could. "Help me, or I shall drown!"

The stranger came slowly up to the bank. He was a tall, solemn man in black clothes.

"Dear, dear!" said the stranger. "What a foolish boy you are! Now how did you get into such difficulties? Surely you knew that the water was too deep for you. Did your dear father and mother never tell you not to go into deep water until you could swim? Now if you were a strong swimmer like me—"

And so he went on preaching at Tom until the poor boy was almost drowned. But Tom managed to find a place where the water was not so deep, and was able to scramble to the bank.

"You might have helped me," he said, when he had got his breath again, "instead of giving me a lecture. You could have done that after I was safe on shore! "

A helping hand is better than a sermon.

FARMER AND SONS

HERE WAS once an old farmer who had worked all his life growing grapes in his vineyard. He had done very well for his wife and their three sons. But at last it was near the time when he would die, and he wanted to teach his sons how to be good farmers. He wasn't at all sure that they really knew how important it is to work hard. So he called them to him one evening and said:

"My boys, it may be that I haven't much longer to live. But before I die, I want you to know that there is great treasure in my vineyard. Promise me you will remember that when I am gone."

The three young men promised; and not long after that, their father died. Then they remembered what he had said, and began to look for the treasure he had left them in the vineyard. They pictured in their minds much coin, or silver plate, or things of that sort. How hard they worked in the hot sun, digging round the vines, turning over the soil with fork and spade, or going over every inch of ground with a hoe.

Well, the three brothers spent a month at least turning over the soil in that vineyard, but not so much as a penny piece could they find. At last they gave up, thinking their father must have been wandering in his mind. But soon the grapes began to appear, and although it was not a good year for other farmers, their grapes were bigger than any that had been grown before in that part of the country. When the grapes were ripe, how big and juicy they were! The brothers took them to the market, and were amazed at the high price they fetched. So now they understood what their father had meant by the great treasure he had left them in the vineyard. They saw that all their hard work had not been wasted, for it had made the grapes grow as they had never grown before.

Hard work brings prosperity.

WOLF AND HOUSE-DOG

THE NIGHT was very cold, and the full moon shone with a frosty glitter. Wolf was very, very hungry. He was lean and tired as he trotted through the woods with his tongue hanging out, ready to drop dead with misery and starvation. Presently up came House-dog and said "Good evening."

Wolf looked at House-dog and saw that he was fat and comfortable and well-fed. So he asked House-dog if he knew where he could find food.

"Oh, there's always food where I live," answered House-dog. "My master gives me plenty of scraps whenever I want them, and sometimes a big juicy bone."

"Master?" said Wolf. "What's that?"

"The man I live with," said House-dog. "I don't have to do much. Just scare away thieves in the night, and go out hunting when master wants to. It's a fine life. You ought to try it."

Wolf didn't need to hear any more. The life of House-dog sounded so very comfortable and safe, and besides, he was so very, very hungry. So he trotted along beside House-dog to see if House-dog's master would take him in.

Then just as they came to the edge of the wood, and were getting near the village, Wolf noticed a mark on House-dog's neck. He stopped, and House-dog stopped too. Wolf pointed his paw at the mark.

"What's that?" asked Wolf.

"What's what?" said House-dog.

"That mark."

"That? Oh, it's just a mark. I got it from the chain."

"Chain?" said Wolf. "Do you mean that your master puts a chain round your neck?"

"Sometimes," said House-dog. "I don't mind much. I'm used to it. Besides, he only chains me up sometimes. He always lets me out at night."

"Never mind," said Wolf. "That's enough for me. You can keep your nice scraps and your bones and your hunting with your master. But if ever I had a chain round my neck, I should die. I may be hungry, but at least I'm free. Good-bye, House-dog."

And with that, Wolf turned round and went back into the woods, leaving House-dog to return home.

Freedom is better than comfort.

ANT AND DOVE

THE ANT was THIRSTY, and going to a pool to drink, she fell in and was almost drowned. Now it happened that a dove was sitting on the branch of a tree overhanging the water. With her sharp eyes she saw the danger that Ant was in, and dropped a leaf, which alighted on the pool. It fell just in front of Ant, who quickly climbed on to it and floated to safety on the bank.

At that very moment a birdcatcher came along with his net, and was just spreading it out to catch the dove. Ant saw what he was trying to do, and noticing that the birdcatcher went barefoot, he bit him in the heel. It was not a very savage bite, but it was the worst that Ant could do; and it was enough to make the birdcatcher jump in the air with surprise. He lost hold of his net, so Dove was just able to escape with her life.

One good turn deserves another.

THE BALD KNIGHT

THERE WAS once a Knight who, as he grew old, lost all of his hair. His head had become as bald as a duck's egg. He didn't want everyone to see how bald he was, so he had a wig made—a fine wig with long curling tresses.

The very first day he put it on, he went hunting with a company of lords and ladies. Away they went over the green fields and the forest, with the hounds racing on ahead, and a gay blowing of horns. The Knight was proud of his new wig, as he cantered along on his black horse.

"How handsome they must all think me!" he said to himself.

Presently the hounds lost the scent, and most of the company gathered together under a grove of oak trees till they could pick it up once more. The King rode up to join them. Then a terrible thing happened. He passed under a tree, and as he did so, his wig was caught on a branch and pulled off over his head in full view of everyone. How they laughed, and how foolish the poor knight looked, after thinking himself so handsome! There he sat on his black horse, while the fine curly wig hung above his head on the oak branch.

The Knight could not help seeing the fun, so he laughed as merrily as everyone else.

"Why," he said almost rolling off his horse with amusement, "how could I expect a wig to stay on my head, when my own hair wouldn't!"

When others laugh at us, it is best to laugh with them.

FOX AND STORK

F OX AND Stork met one day beside the lake. Stork lifted his long beak out of the water and said, "Good day."

"Good day to you," answered Fox with a low bow. "And a very fine day it is. You're just the fellow I was looking for. Why not come along to my place this evening and have supper?"

"With pleasure," answered Stork. "I'll be with you at dusk."

Now Reynard thought he would play a trick on Stork and make a fool of him, when he could tell all the other animals about it, and show them what a clever fellow he was. He made some rich soup, and served it in two shallow dishes. He took one himself, and set the other in front of Stork.

"I think you'll enjoy this," said Reynard, as soon as Stork was ready for supper. "Don't wait, my dear Stork, or the soup will be cold."

He licked his own supper up with much enjoyment, and watched poor Stork trying to drink from the shallow dish with his long thin beak. Of course Stork had almost no supper.

"Aren't you enjoying it?" asked Fox.

Stork answered that he wasn't feeling specially hungry, and had really enjoyed his supper immensely. Before he went, he asked Reynard to come to supper with him the following day.

"With the greatest of pleasure!" answered Reynard.

Next evening, when Fox came to supper with Stork, he found that once more the meal was soup, and very good it smelt. But Stork had

The Fox and the Stork

served it in two tall jars with narrow necks. Stork dipped his long beak into his jar, but Reynard got scarcely a drop and had to be content with licking the top. He was very angry indeed, and went home without saying good night.

But afterwards Reynard saw that he had been treated just as he deserved—and he did *not* boast to the other animals of how he had tricked Stork.

*Those who play tricks on others
must expect to be tricked themselves.*

DONKEY CARRYING SALT

THERE WAS once a shopkeeper who heard that salt could be bought very cheaply down by the sea. So he took a great basket, tied it to his donkey, and set out for the shore. He filled the basket to the very top with good white salt. Then he tied the lid on securely and started for home, leading Donkey behind him with a rope round his neck. Donkey didn't like the heavy load, but he struggled along with it, until they came to a river which they had to cross. Donkey slipped on a rock in the middle of the river, and fell over. When he got to his feet again, the water had washed away most of the salt, so of course he found the load much lighter.

"What a bit of luck!" said Donkey to himself. "I should never have thought of that."

Next day the shopkeeper went to the sea to get more salt. Once again he filled up the basket and set off, leading Donkey along by the rope. When they came to the river, Donkey remembered what had happened the day before, and slipped over on purpose. Once more they reached home without any salt.

But the shopkeeper had seen what happened.

"We'll put an end to tricks like that!" he said to himself.

Next time, when he got to the sea, he loaded up the basket, not with salt but with sponges. Donkey didn't know the difference, and once again he managed to tumble into the water on purpose, in order to get rid of his load.

But the sponges weren't washed away. They had been dry to start with, and now they were full of water and very heavy.

Poor Donkey struggled home with the load of sponges. He was nearly dead with the weight of them.

"That just shows," said his friend Barn-owl, when he told her about it, "that if you try the same trick too often, you're sure to be found out."

Too much cunning does us no good.

WIND AND SUN

THERE WAS once a time when Wind and Sun had an argument about which was the stronger.

"I am the stronger," boasted Wind, puffing out his cheeks and blowing so hard that every leaf on the trees shook. "You sit up there, Sun, and do nothing but shine—that is, when I don't blow the clouds across the sky. When that happens, you can't even be seen! Of course I'm the stronger."

"Don't be too sure," answered Sun calmly, filling the air with his warm radiance. "I'll tell you what. We'll have a contest, shall we?"

"Certainly," said Wind. "Then everyone will know, once and for all, who is the stronger. What shall the contest be?"

"See that fellow over there?" said Sun, gazing across the countryside towards a winding, white road. Along it walked a traveller with a cloak about his shoulders.

"I see him," said Wind.

"Well then, let's see which of us can get his cloak off first."

"With all my heart!" agreed Wind. "That's easy. I'll have his cloak off his back in no time."

So saying, he began to blow. "Phoo—oo—oo!" The traveller on the road took no notice. But Wind had scarcely begun. He blew harder, and then harder still, till the water of the lakes turned to great waves, and the trees were bent almost double, and the birds in the air were dashed hither and thither with the force of the gale. But the traveller, instead of taking his cloak off, only held it closer round him;

and the harder Wind blew, the tighter he clutched it. It was no good. Even when Wind roared like a thousand demons, and blew so as to snap the branches from the stoutest oaks, he could not get the traveller's cloak off his back. At last Wind was tired out and could blow no more. It was Sun's turn. By now the sky was all covered over with dark storm-clouds, but as soon as Wind stopped blowing they gently drifted apart, and Sun shone warmly down over the green fields. Warmer and warmer grew the air under his pleasant beams, and soon the traveller unbuttoned his cloak and let it hang loosely about him. Thanks to Sun's kindly heat he was soon glad to take it off altogether and carry it over his arm.

"There!" said Sun "Which of us got it off tell me that."

Wind only growled and said nothing. But he knew he was beaten. Sun was the stronger after all.

Gentleness achieves more than violence.

JOAN

HERE WAS once a country girl called Joan. She worked hard at her old mother's dairy-farm, and very well she managed it. But Joan was a little vain—or, as people used to say, she gave herself airs. One evening she was walking back home through the meadows carrying a big can of milk on her head. She didn't hurry, for the evening was pleasant, and she liked to stroll along, turning things over in her mind.

"Let me see," said Joan to herself, "I shall get four or five shillings for this milk, and with that money I shall be able to get two dozen— no, three dozen eggs. That'll make three hundred, all told. Now if my three hundred eggs hatch out—well, I suppose some will turn out bad, and some will get taken by vermin—suppose I get two hundred and fifty young chicks. I'll sell them for pullets," she went on. "No, I'll keep them till they're full grown. Then poultry will be dear. Yes, I'll sell forty or fifty of them at least, and then I'll be able to go into town and buy myself a new dress. A silk dress it shall be. No, satin. I look best in satin. And what colour shall it be? Pink? No, not pink, nor yellow neither. *All* the girls will be wearing yellow. I want to be different. White? No, not white: that Susan Huckaby always dresses in white, and I don't want to look a fright like her. Nasty, stuck-up thing! No, it shall be green—that's it. Green satin! I shall look a picture in green satin, and everyone will notice me."

Joan smiled with happiness at the thought of everyone admiring her in the new dress she was going to buy. Then she went on, saying to herself:

"I shall wear it at the fair, so I will, and all the young fellows will want to dance with me. There'll be Tom, and Jack, and even that handsome Oliver that Susan is always running after. But I shan't have one of them. I shall just toss my head and have nothing to do with them. That's what I'll do—I'll toss my head!"

And here Joan was so taken up with her thoughts that she forgot all about the can of milk. She gave a haughty toss of her head, just for practice, and down fell the can, and all the milk was spilt in the grass. So poor Joan had to go home without anything to sell. The wonderful dream she had been enjoying all vanished like spilt milk.

Don't count your chickens before they are hatched.

CROW AND PITCHER

THE SUMMER was very hot. There had been no rain for weeks. All the ponds and rivers were dry. Crow had spent a whole day looking for water. He flew here and there just for a beakful to quench his thirst. Not a drop could he find.

"Oh dear, oh dear!" thought Crow. "If I don't have some water soon, I shall die."

And it was true, for many of his brothers were already dead from thirst.

At last he noticed a pitcher standing in one corner of a yard. A housewife had been drawing water from the pump and had been called indoors. It was a heavy earthenware pitcher. Crow lighted on the edge of it and looked in. Yes, there was water in it. He stretched out his neck and reached down with his beak. The water was too low, but get some he must, or die.

Tired as he was, he hammered at the pitcher with his beak, trying to break it. But he had little strength, and the pitcher was too hard for him. Then he tried to knock it over. He stood on the ground and hit it with his wings; he ran against it, and flew against it, but it was no use. He could not knock it over.

At last, half dead with his efforts, he saw a heap of pebbles in another corner of the yard. He picked them up, one by one, and dropped them into the pitcher. He heard each one splash into the water, and then went back for more. It was as much as he could do to lift the pebbles and carry them across the yard.

Then at last there were so many in the pitcher that the water rose near enough to the top for him to be able to reach it with his beak. How greedily he drank! Of course he didn't get very much water, but it was enough to save his life.

Skill and patience achieve more than force.

ZORIAN THE STAR-GAZER

T HERE WAS once an astronomer called Zorian, a very clever man with bright, thoughtful eyes and a long white beard. Every day he would read books about the sun, the moon and the other heavenly bodies; and at night he would gaze up at the stars and write down signs and figures on parchment scrolls. But it was not easy for Zorian to gaze at the stars from his house in the middle of the city, so on dark nights he used to walk out into the fields where he could get a better view.

One winter night, when there was not a cloud in the sky, and no moon to dim the glittering of the stars, he wandered out of the town in a direction he had not taken before. He was making for a slight hill that lay not far off. As he went, he kept his bright eyes fixed on the planets overhead. So intent was he on his stargazing that he strayed a little to one side of the path. Suddenly he lost his footing and toppled over the edge of a well. There was a great splash as he hit the icy water, and in a second he was up to his neck in it.

"Help!" cried Zorian as soon as he could get his breath. "Come quickly, somebody, or I shall drown—or freeze to death! Help, help!"

As luck would have it, a soldier on his way back to town heard the astronomer's cries. Running to the well, he hauled the unfortunate Zorian out of the water, half dead with cold and fright. His teeth were chattering with cold and the icy water dripped from his beard.

They went back to the city together, and by the lighted window of a house the soldier recognized the man he had saved.

"Why, if it isn't the old fellow who roams about the streets with his eyes in the top of his head!" he exclaimed. "If you ask my advice, sir, in future you'll forget about the stars and look where you're going."

Zorian thanked the soldier for his help and went home.

Those who don't see what is in front of them
run into danger.

THE TWO TRAVELLERS

TWO MEN were travelling through a wood to reach town before nightfall. It was getting dark. They kept together for company. Soon there was a sound of heavy footsteps in the undergrowth, and suddenly a great brown bear stood in the pathway in front of them.

Without a thought for the other, the first traveller ran for the nearest tree and climbed high into the branches. As soon as he was safe, he looked down to see what was happening to his companion.

The second traveller ran too, but he tripped over a root and fell to the ground. He had no time to climb a tree, so he stayed where he was, pretending to be dead. He knew that bears will not touch a dead body. He kept as still as death, never moving a finger. His eyes were closed, and he scarcely dared to breathe.

The bear stooped down over him and nosed him all over. In particular, he sniffed at the traveller's face. But there was no sign of life in him, and soon the bear lumbered away into the woods and was seen no more.

As soon as he saw it was quite safe, the first traveller climbed down from his tree. The second traveller had got to his feet, and the first said to him:

"That was a close thing! I thought he had got you then. I'm glad you came to no harm, but tell me—what did the bear say to you when he put his nose to your ear? It looked to me as if he was whispering some secret."

"That was no secret," said the second traveller. "He only told me to take care who I travel with, and not trust a man who runs away when his companion is in danger."

So he left the first traveller and went on alone.

Avoid a companion who cannot be trusted.

KING LION IS ILL

HE LION was ill, so very ill that he was too weak to come out of his den and hunt for food. He moaned and groaned, and a little bird, hopping about near the mouth of the den, heard him. So the bird flew through the jungle crying out, "King Lion is ill! King Lion is ill!"

The other animals were sorry to hear this, and one by one they went to his den to visit him and say how sorry they were. Some of them took presents. Goat brought some herbs he had found on a hillside, and Antelope took some fruit he had gathered from the bushes.

Well, of course, when the animals came right into Lion's own den, he was able to fall upon them easily and kill them for his food. One by one, as each animal went in, he was put to death by clever King Lion and eaten. At last Reynard the Fox passed by the cave where the king was lying, and he called into the cave:

"Good day, Your Majesty, I trust you are beginning to feel better."

"A little better, thank you," answered Lion. "Why did you not come sooner, like all my other subjects, to say how sorry you are that I have been ill?"

"I have only just heard the sad news," said Reynard.

"Well, better late than never," growled Lion. "Come in, my dear fellow, and wish me good health."

"Not just now, thank you," said Fox slyly. "Some other time, perhaps. I really ought to be getting home. I've just noticed something that tells me it would be extremely unwise for me to visit Your

Majesty in his royal den."

"And what is that, pray?" said Lion, somewhat annoyed.

"Well, you see," said Reynard. "I observe a number of footprints in the sand outside your den. Here is Goat's footprint, and here is Antelope's—and yes, here is Rabbit's, I think, and here is Donkey's."

"What of it?" asked Lion. "They have all had the good manners to come and bring me gifts. Naturally they left their footmarks outside."

"Ah yes, Your Majesty," said Reynard with a little laugh, "but you see, all the footprints point into your cave. I see none coming out!"

So saying, Fox made a deep bow and vanished hastily in the direction of his lair.

Cunning is defeated by greater cunning.

MICE AND CAT

THE MICE all met together one day, very secretly in a safe, dry cellar, to talk about Cat. They had been having a dreadful time lately. Cat was always on the prowl. It seemed that mistress gave him no food and little milk, so that he hunted the mice day and night. They never had a moment's peace. Only last night he had killed no fewer than five of them. So you can understand that the meeting of mice was a very angry one; if the cellar had not been such a safe cellar, Cat would certainly have heard their angry squeakings.

"I suggest," said one mouse, "that we all live down here. Cat doesn't seem to know about this place."

"That's all very well," said another, "but we've got to go out sometimes and look for food."

"Suppose we move to a different house?" said a third mouse.

"Yes, but which?" someone objected. "There are plenty of mice in most of the houses round here, and they won't welcome us!"

"Besides, there's good eating here."

"Yes, we're used to it. This is our home! Why should we move? Let Cat move."

"That's right," said several mice. "Let's get rid of Cat."

"Poison his milk!" said one mouse.

"Set fire to his tail!" suggested another.

"Attack him all together, and bite him to pieces!"

The meeting was getting nowhere, and the mice had become very disorderly, as well as noisy. Then the smallest mouse of all hopped on

The Mice and the Cat

to an old flower-pot so that he could be seen, and piped up in a high nervous voice :

"May I speak, please? I think I've got an idea."

One mouse laughed but another said, "Go on, young 'un!" and others said, "Let him speak" and "Quiet, everyone!" and "Out with it, then!"

The very smallest mouse cleared his throat and began. "The trouble is," he said, "we never know when Cat's coming. He's so quiet and stealthy, he just creeps up on us before we catch sight or smell of him."

"That's right. But how can we help it?"

"Quiet, you, and let the little 'un go on!"

"Well," went on the smallest mouse, "I know where there's an old rusty bell. It's not very big, but it makes a good clear ring when you shake it. I know 'cos me and my sister plays with it sometimes. Well, I thought that if we were to tie that bell round Cat's neck so that he couldn't get it off, we'd always know when he was coming, and we could get out of the way in time."

This seemed to be a wonderful idea. Why had no one thought of it before? Of course! Tie a bell to Cat, and he would never trouble them any more. There was loud cheering and squeaking for joy, and everyone shouted "Hooray! That's the best idea so far. Let's have a vote on it!" And several mice shook the smallest mouse by the paw and slapped him on the back till he was quite dazed and fell off the flower-pot.

"Very well," shouted the most important mouse, rapping on the floor with a nutshell, "let's take a vote. Paws up for tying a bell round Cat's neck!"

"Just one moment," said the very oldest mouse, getting shakily to his feet and speaking to the meeting for the first time. So far he had just sat quietly in a corner. He was very old and very grey, and all the mice knew he was extremely wise, except when he was asleep, as he nearly always was.

"I think," said he, "this is an excellent plan. If we could attach this bell to our enemy, we should indeed, as our young friend has pointed out, be warned of his approach and be able to get away in time. But before we vote on this proposal, there is just one question I should like to ask—and I think we ought to consider it most seriously."

"Out with it!" said a mouse. "Get it off your chest, Gaffer!"

The oldest mouse took no notice of the interruption, for being rather deaf, he had scarcely heard it.

"Which of you," he went on, speaking slowly and gravely—"which of you is going to tie this bell around Cat's neck?"

Nobody said a word. There was not a sound. You could have heard a corn-seed drop.

"Dash my whiskers!" thought the smallest mouse to himself. "I never thought of that."

As for the oldest mouse of all, he sat down again in his corner, and fell asleep immediately.

And to this very day, mice have never known how to get the better of Cat.

Before deciding on a plan, find out if it can be carried out.

THE WOODCUTTER AND THE TREES

MATTHEW THE Woodcutter needed a new handle for his axe. So he went into the great forest and said to all the trees: "I have broken the handle of my axe, and have come to ask you for a new one. Will one of you give me a straight, sturdy piece of wood for what I need?"

The trees agreed to this small request, and the noblest of them put their heads together to decide which of all the trees in the forest should sacrifice itself to make Matthew a new handle for his axe.

"What about the pine?" said the oak. "He is a good straight tree."

"Not at all," said the pine, who had overheard him. "What about the elm?"

"I refuse," said the elm. "I would make a very poor handle. I tell you what, though. Let's make the ash surrender himself. He's a plain, homely little tree, and he can't very well object."

So they made the ash give himself up to the woodcutter, and no sooner had Matthew made a new handle from the wood of the ash than he began laying about him in all directions. He cut down one tree after another, and all day long the forest rang with the noise of the blows.

"Alas!" said the oak to the cedar. "Now I see what we have done. It will be our turn before long. He won't spare us. If only we hadn't sacrificed the poor ash, but stuck together and refused to give this woodcutter the means to destroy us all!"

When great people sacrifice the poor and humble,
they make trouble for themselves in the end.

WOLF AND GOAT

THE WOLF WAS roaming the green slopes at the foot of some craggy hills. He was hungry, and nowhere could he find any prey, for the goats that fed in those hills had learnt to keep well out of his way. Presently he spied a goat nibbling the grass among some rocks which were too steep and dangerous for any creature but a goat.

Wolf looked up and called out:

"Hi, Goat! What are you doing up there?"

"Eating my dinner," answered Goat.

"What's the grass like?"

"Not bad," said Goat.

"You ought to be careful," called Wolf. "You may miss your footing among all those loose stones. Then think what would happen to you. It's not safe."

"Oh, I can manage all right," said Goat, with his mouth full. "I'm used to scrambling among the rocks."

"Yes, but you should taste the grass down here," Wolf went on. "It's much sweeter and greener. Come on down and try it."

"Thanks very much, Wolf dear," answered Goat. "But I think I'll stay where I am. You know, I have an idea it's your dinner you're thinking about—not mine!"

And he scrambled a little higher, just to be on the safe side, and went on with his nibbling.

Don't always trust those who say they want to help you.

COCK AND FOX

THE COCK Chanticleer was perched on the farmyard fence. His red comb and his feathers shone in the sun, and he was very proud of himself as he gazed down upon his slaves, the hens. Just as he was telling himself for the twentieth time what a handsome fellow he was, Reynard the Fox came into the yard and caught sight of him.

"What a fine fat cock!" he said to himself. "Now wouldn't he make a good dinner for me and my wife and the little ones? I wonder how I can get hold of him. I must be careful not to frighten him away."

So the fox trotted carelessly towards Chanticleer and said:

"Good morning, my dear young fellow. I don't hear you singing today. Is anything the matter? I remember your father well. He was a wonderful singer. I bet you can't sing like him."

"Much better," answered Chanticleer boastfully. "Just you listen to me."

"Wait a moment," said Reynard. "Your late lamented father had a special way of singing. He used to shut his eyes tight, lift up his head and then start. Like that, he did it beautifully. I never heard anything so good in my life!"

"Then I will do the same," said Chanticleer. "If father did it, so can I."

So saying, he stretched out his neck, took a deep breath and closed his eyes tightly. He was just going to begin crowing when Reynard gave a mighty spring and seized him by the throat. Then he ran swiftly out of the farmyard.

What a terrible shock for Chanticleer!

"Oh dear," he said to himself, with his head hanging out of Reynard's jaws. "Now I'm done for. How silly I was to listen to the fox's flattery!"

Reynard had to run hard, for the farmer and his men had seen him steal the cock and were now running after him with their rakes and hay-forks, shouting angrily.

"Drop that bird!" cried the farmer. "You're a thieving rogue to steal my cock."

"Mr. Fox," said the cock in a thin little voice. "Do you hear them shouting? Why don't you tell them that I belong to you now, not them?"

To Reynard this seemed a good idea. He stopped, turned round, and shouted to the farmer:

"This is my bird, you old fool, not yours!"

But as he opened his jaws to speak, Chanticleer slipped away and flew high into a tree out of reach. He was almost dead with fright, but he was safe. The fox ran away into the woods as fast as his legs could take him.

"What a fool I was to open my mouth!" he said, when he was safe at home. "If I hadn't talked, I'd have been enjoying a good meal by now."

And he determined to have more sense in future.

It is sometimes better to keep our mouths shut.

GOAT AND GOAT-HERD

A HERD OF goats was being driven slowly home to be milked. A boy was following them, trying to get them to move faster, as he wanted his supper. One goat strayed away from his companions to get at some fine long grass that grew a little distance from the path.

"Get back!" shouted the goat-herd "Get back, there, I say!"

But Goat took no notice.

The boy called and whistled, but still Goat would not return to the herd.

At last the boy lost his patience and picked up a stone. He flung it at Goat, hoping to drive him back. But the stone struck one of Goat's horns and broke off the end of it.

"That's done it," said the goat-herd. "Master won't half be angry with me if he knows I've been throwing stones at his animals."

He ran up to Goat and spoke to him.

"Don't say anything about this, Goat," he pleaded. "Don't tell master, or he'll punish me. I didn't mean to hit you, only scare you a bit. I won't do it again."

"That's all very well," said Goat. "But even if I say nothing, your master will see my broken horn. I'm afraid he's bound to find out."

Facts speak louder than words.

TOM AND THE PITCHER

OM KNEW where his mother kept the tall pitcher full of figs and nuts. When no one was in the kitchen, he lifted it down from the shelf and put it on the table. Then he pushed his hand into it and grabbed as many figs and nuts as he could hold. What a splendid feed he would have, and how he loved the green figs and the plump, ripe nuts!

But he had filled his hand so full that he couldn't get it out past the narrow neck. Try as he might, his bulging hand stuck fast, but he would not let go any of the figs and nuts.

"What a miserable boy I am!" said Tom, beginning to cry. "It's not fair!"

He began to wail so piteously that the serving-woman came in and asked what the matter was. Between his sobs Tom told her.

"Why, you greedy boy!" scolded the servant. "If you weren't in such a hurry, you'd drop half the figs and not try to get so many at a time."

Greed doesn't pay.

DONKEY COCK AND LION

THE DONKEY AND the Cock lived together in a farmyard. Very contented they were, until one day King Lion came along. He looked at Donkey and saw that he was fat and healthy, so he thought he would make a meal of him.

Now there is one thing that King Lion is frightened of—and that is the crowing of a cock. Well, just as Lion was going to spring into the farmyard, it happened that Cock began to crow.

"Cock-a-doodle-do!" he cried, at the moment when Donkey first caught sight of King Lion. Lion, hearing the noise, stopped still, then turned away, and began to slink off.

"Fancy that!" cried Donkey. "What a coward Lion must be to run away from the noise of a bird. I must be braver than Lion, for I hear Cock crow two or three times a day, and it doesn't scare me at all. Suppose I go and chase Lion myself! What fun it'll be to see him run off."

So, laughing to himself, Donkey galloped out of the farmyard in the direction taken by King Lion. This time there was no cock-a-doodle to frighten Lion. So of course he turned on Donkey and sprang at him with a fierce growl. And that was the end of Donkey!

Pride and stupidity end in ruin.

The Lion and the Donkey
Go Hunting

As everyone knows, the lion is a mighty hunter. But even the king of the beasts at times grows tired of hunting for his food. So once a lion made an agreement with a donkey to go hunting together.

The plan was that they were to proceed to a certain cave where a herd of wild goats were accustomed to take shelter. The lion was to take a position near the mouth of the cave while the donkey went inside and made such a hideous noise by braying and kicking and stamping that the terrified animals would run right into the lion's trap

The plan worked beautifully. The lion caught and killed and devoured several goats, and after his hearty meal he stretched out to take his ease.

Just then the donkey, anxious to claim his share of the noble victory, came up to the reclining lion and said: "How was that for a job? Didn't I give those goats the worst of it? And what do you think of the noise I made? Wasn't it wonderful?"

"Yes, indeed," replied the lion sleepily. "As a matter of fact, if I hadn't known you to be only a donkey, I think I would have been scared myself."

Braggarts usually get themselves laughed at in the end.

ANDROCLES AND THE LION

THERE WAS ONCE a slave named Androcles who was cruelly treated by his master. When the opportunity came he escaped to the forest. In his wanderings he came upon a lion. His first instinct was to turn about and flee. Then he noticed that the lion seemed to be in great distress and was moaning and whimpering piteously.

As the slave came near, the lion put out his paw, which was swollen and bleeding. A large thorn had penetrated one of the lion's toes, and this was the cause of all the animal's discomfort. Quickly Androcles pulled out the thorn and bound up the wounded paw. To show his gratitude the lion licked the man's hand like a dog, and then he led him to his cave for a shelter. Every day, after his wound had healed, he would go hunting in the forest and return with fresh meat for his master's refreshment.

But one day, when Androcles and the lion went out together, they were both captured and taken to the city to be used in the circus. The slave was to be thrown to the lion, after the animal had been kept without food for several days to make him more ferocious.

The Emperor and all his court came to the arena to view the spectacle. The despairing slave was unchained and led out into the amphitheater before the Emperor's box. Then the lion was let loose, and rushed bounding and roaring toward his victim. But as soon as he came near Androcles he recognized his friend. To the surprise of the audience, the lion seemed to fawn upon the slave whom they had expected to see torn to shreds by the savage beast. Pleased by this unusual spectacle the Emperor summoned Androcles to him, and the slave told him the whole story. Thereupon the slave was pardoned and freed, and the lion set loose to return to his native forest.

Gratitude is a quality not limited to man.

The Milkmaid and her Pail

THE MILKMAID was on her way to market, carrying a pail of milk on the top of her head. As she walked along the road in the early morning she began to turn in her mind what she would do with the money she would receive for the milk.

"I shall buy some hens from a neighbour," said she to herself, "and they will lay eggs every day which I shall sell to the pastor's wife. And with the egg money I'll buy myself a new frock and ribbon. Green they should be, for green becomes my complexion best. And in this lovely green gown I will go to the fair. All the young men will strive to have me for a partner. I shall pretend that I do not see them. When they become too insistent I shall disdainfully toss my head—like this."

As the milkmaid spoke she tossed her head back, and down came the pail of milk, spilling all over the ground. And so all her imaginary happiness vanished, and nothing was left but an empty pail and the promise of a scolding when she returned home.

Do not count your chickens before they are hatched.

The Boy and the Filberts

THE BOY put his hand into a pitcher which contained a goodly quantity of figs and filberts. Greedily he clutched as many as his fist could possibly hold. But when he tried to pull it out, the narrowness of the neck of the vessel prevented him.

Unwilling to lose any of the nuts, yet unable to draw out his hand, the lad burst into tears, bitterly bewailing his hard fortune. An honest fellow standing near by gave him this wise and reasonable advice: "Grasp only half the quantity, my boy, and you will easily succeed."

Half a loaf is better than no bread.

THE SWALLOW'S ADVICE

THE FARMER was sowing his field with hemp seeds while a swallow and some other birds sat on the fence watching him. "Beware of that man," said the swallow solemnly.

"Why should we be afraid of him?" asked the other birds.

"That farmer is sowing hemp seed," replied the swallow. "It is most important that you pick every seed he drops. You will live to regret it if you don't."

But, of course, the silly birds paid no heed to the swallow's advice. So, with the coming of the spring rains, the hemp grew up. And one day the hemp was made into cord, and of the cord, nets were made. And many of the birds that had despised the swallow's advice were caught in the nets made of the very hemp that was grown from the seeds they had failed to pick up.

Unless the seed of evil is destroyed
it will grow up to destroy us.

THE DOG INVITED TO DINNER

A GENTLEMAN, having prepared a great feast, invited his good friend to supper. It chanced that on that same day the gentleman's dog met the friend's dog. "Come," said he, "my good fellow, and sup with us tonight."

The dog was delighted with the invitation, and as he stood watching the dinner being brought from the kitchen, he licked his chops and said: "My, but that smells good. This is luck, indeed! I shall make the most of my opportunity and eat my fill tonight, for I may have nothing to eat tomorrow."

As he spoke thus to himself he wagged his tail and gave a sly look at his friend who had invited him. But his tail wagging to and fro caught the attention of the cook, who, seeing a stranger, straightaway seized him by the legs and threw him out the window.

When he reached the ground he set off yelping down the street. Thereupon the neighbours' dogs ran up to him and asked him how he had enjoyed his supper. "To tell you the truth," said he with a sorry smile, "we drank so deep that I can't even tell you which way I got out of the house."

They who enter by the back stairs
may expect to be shown out at the window.

The Bundle of Sticks

THERE WAS once a wise farmer whose quarrelsome family drove him almost to distraction. He strove in vain to recon cile his bickering sons with words of good counsel. Then one day he called his sons to his room. Before him lay a bundle of sticks which he had tied together to form a fagot.

Each one of his sons in turn was commanded by the farmer to take up the fagot and break it in two. They all tried, but tried in vain. Then, untying the bundle, the farmer gave them the sticks to break one by one. This, of course, they did with the greatest ease.

Then said the farmer: "My sons, by this example you all can see that as long as you remain united, you are a match for all your enemies. But once you quarrel and become separated, then you are destroyed."

In union there is strength.

The Heifer and the Ox

HERE WAS once a young heifer who, never having felt the yoke, gambled about in the fields as free as the wind. With her tail in the air she frisked up to the old ox who was pulling a plough for the farmer.

"How foolish you are," she said to the toiling ox, "to work so hard all day long. Why don't you do as I do, enjoy life, go and come as you will, instead or submitting to such drudgery day in, day out?"

The old ox said nothing, but went on with his work. When evening came he was turned loose by the farmer, and he went over to the village altar where the priests were preparing to offer the heifer as a sacrifice.

The ox approached the heifer and said: "How do you feel about it now? You must know now why you were allowed to live in idleness. As for me, I had rather my neck felt the weight of the yoke than of the knife."

He laughs best that laughs last.

THE OLD MAN AND DEATH

THE OLD MAN, stooped by age and hard work, was gathering sticks in the forest. As he hobbled painfully along he thought of his troubles and began to feel very sorry for himself.

With a hopeless gesture he threw his bundle of sticks upon the ground and groaned: "Life is too hard. I cannot bear it any longer. If only Death would come and take me!"

Even as the words were out of his mouth, Death, in the form of a skeleton in a black robe, stood before him. "I heard you call me, sir," he said. "What can I do for you?"

"Please, sir," replied the old man, "could you please help me to put this bundle of sticks back on my shoulder again!"

How sorry we should be
if many of our wishes were granted.

The Porcupine and the Snakes

HE PORCUPINE had selected a comfortable cave for his home only to find it already occupied by a family of snakes. "Would it be agreeable if I used one corner of your cave to spend the winter?" he asked. The snakes very generously offered to share their home with the porcupine, and he moved in, curled up in a ball, stuck out all his prickly quills, and settled down for the winter.

It was not very long, however, before the snakes realized that they had made a mistake, for every time one of them moved he would prick himself on one of the visitor's quills.

After bearing this discomfort for a time the snakes got up their courage to complain to the porcupine.

"That's just too bad," said their guest. "I am most comfortable here. But if you snakes aren't satisfied, why don't you move out?" And he curled up once more and resumed his nap.

It is safer to know one's guest
before offering him hospitality.

THE FISHERMAN PIPING

THERE WAS once a fisherman who enjoyed playing on the bagpipes as much as he did fishing. He sat down on the riverbank and played a gay tune, hoping that the fish would be attracted and jump ashore.

When nothing happened, he took a casting net, threw it into the water, and soon drew it forth filled with fish. Then, as the fish danced and flopped about in the net on shore, the fisherman shook his head and said: "Since you would not dance when I piped, I will have none of your dancing now!"

*To do the right thing at the right season
is a great art.*

THE GNAT AND THE BULL

HERE WAS once a silly gnat who kept buzzing about the head of a bull. Finally he settled himself down upon one of the bull's horns.

"Pardon me, Mr. Bull," he said, "if I am inconveniencing you. If my weight in any way is burdensome to you, pray say so, and I will be off in a moment."

"Oh, never trouble your head about that," replied the bull. "It is all the same to me whether you go or stay. To tell the truth, I was not even aware that you were there."

The smaller the mind the greater the conceit.

THE LARK AND HER YOUNG ONES

T HE LARK, WHO had her nest of young ones in a wheat field, had to leave them each day to go out and hunt for food for them. As the wheat ripened, the mother, expecting the arrival of the reapers, left word that the young larks should report to her all the news they heard.

One day, while she was absent, the farmer came to view his crop. "It is high time," he called to his son, "that our grain is cut. Go, tell all our neighbours to come early in the morning to help us reap it." When the mother lark came her children told her what they had heard, and begged her to remove them to a place of safety. "There's plenty of time," said she. "If friend farmer waits for his neighbours to help him, there's no danger of the grain being harvested tomorrow."

The next day, the owner came again, and finding the day warmer and the wheat dead-ripe and nothing done, said to his son: "There is not a moment to be lost. We cannot depend upon our neighbours, we must call in all of our relatives. You run now and call all your uncles and cousins and tell them to be here bright and early tomorrow morning to begin the harvest."

In still greater fear, the young larks repeated to the mother the farmer's words when she came home to her nest. "If that is all," she said, "then do not let it frighten you, for relatives always have harvesting of their own to do. But I want you to listen very carefully to what you hear the next time, and be sure to let me know what is said."

The next day while she was away the farmer came as before, and finding the grain almost ready to fall to the ground from over ripeness, and still no one at work, called to his son: "We can't wait for our neighbours and relatives any longer. You and I are going to the barn right now and sharpen our sickles. At dawn tomorrow morning we shall get to work and harvest the grain ourselves."

When the young larks told their mother what they had heard the farmer say, she cried: "Then it is time to be off, indeed. If the master has made up his mind to undertake the work himself, then the grain really will be cut." So the mother lark moved her nest, and the next day the farmer and his son came with their sickles and harvested the wheat.

If you want a task well done, do it yourself:

The Creaking Wheels

SLOWLY and ponderously over the dusty road a yoke oxen were hauling a heavily laden wagon. Each time the wheels turned on their axles they set up a tremendous creaking. Driven almost frantic by the ear-piercing noise, the driver cried: "Wagon, why do you make all this clamour and complaint, when they who are drawing all the weight are silent?"

He who cries loudest is often the least hurt.

THE MONKEY AND THE CAMEL

T A GREAT gathering of all the beasts the monkey got up to entertain his friends by doing a dance. So nimble were his feet and so amusing his gestures and grimaces that all the animals roared with laughter. Even the lion, the King of Beasts, forgot his royal dignity and rolled on the ground with glee.

Only the camel seemed to be bored by the monkey's performance. "I don't see anything so funny in that exhibition," she sniffed. "As a matter of fact, it seems very crude and amateurish to me."

"All right, then," cried all the animals, "suppose you show us what you can do!"

Realizing what she had let herself in for, the camel shambled into the circle, and in no time at all had made herself utterly ridiculous by her awkward and stumbling performance. All the beasts booed her and set upon her with clubs and claws and drove her out into the desert.

Stretch your arm no farther than your sleeve will reach.

THE TREES AND THE AXE

HE WOODMAN came out of the forest one day carrying an axe without any handle! He sat down upon the mossy ground and looked about him rather helplessly.

"What's the trouble, friend woodman?" inquired a friendly old oak.

"I need a handle for my axe," replied the man. "Mostly any piece of wood will do."

After a whispered consultation, the trees good-naturedly offered the woodman a fine piece of tough ashwood for a handle.

But no sooner had the wood chopper fitted the helve with his ax when he set to work on all sides, felling the noblest trees in the wood.

The old oak, witnessing the destruction all about him, whispered to the cedar tree: "If we had not sacrificed our humble neighbour, the ash tree, to please the woodchopper, we might all of us remain standing for ages."

They are foolish who give their enemy
the means of destroying them.

THE MISER

THE MISER, WHO never stopped worrying about the safety of his many possessions, sold all his property and converted it into a huge lump of gold. This he buried in a hole in the ground near his garden wall, and every morning he went to visit it and gloat over the size of it.

The miser's strange behaviour aroused the curiosity of the town thief. Spying upon the rich man from some bushes, the thief saw him place the lump of gold back in the hole and cover it up. As soon as the miser's back was turned, the thief went to the spot, dug up the gold and took it away.

The next morning when the miser came to gloat over his treasure he found nothing but an empty hole. He wept and tore his hair, and so loud were his lamentations that a neighbour came running to see what was the trouble. As soon as he learned the cause of it, he said comfortingly: "You are foolish to distress yourself so over something that was buried in the earth. Take a stone and put it in the hole, and think that it is your lump of gold. You never meant to use it anyway. Therefore it will do you just as much good to fondle a lump of granite as a lump of gold."

The true value of money is not in its possession
but in its use.

THE VAIN CROW

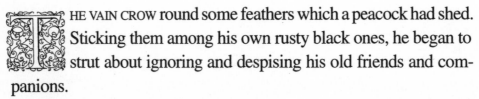

HE VAIN CROW round some feathers which a peacock had shed. Sticking them among his own rusty black ones, he began to strut about ignoring and despising his old friends and companions.

Dressed in his borrowed plumage, he very cockily sought out a flock of peacocks who were walking with stately steps on the park lawn. Instantly detecting the true nature of the intruder, they stripped him of his finery and falling upon him with their sharp beaks, they sent him packing.

The bedraggled Crow, sadder but wiser, betook himself to his former companions, and would have been satisfied to associate with them again. But the crows, remembering how obnoxious he had been with his airs and his vanity, drummed him out of their society. One of those whom he had so lately despised offered him the following advice: "Be contented with what nature made you and you will avoid the contempt of your peers and the punishment of your betters."

Happiness is not to be found in borrowed finery.

THE FIR TREE AND THE BRAMBLE

THE FIR TREE which grew tall and straight over most of the forest trees was boasting one day to a humble Bramble Bush beneath him. His haughtiness and boasting made the Bramble Bush annoyed, and he said: "If I were as tall as you I would not need to put on such airs."

"How can a wretched bramble bush understand the feelings of a tree whose top brushes the clouds," was the haughty reply.

"Just wait," said Bramble. "I hope I am here the day the woodmen come with their sharp axes and saws looking for a tall fir tree. Then, I wager, you will wish you were nothing but a humble, useless bramble bush."

The humble are secure from many dangers
to which the proud are subject.

THE DONKEY'S SHADOW

HE YOUNG man had to make a journey from one city to another, so he hired a donkey and a driver to take him.

The young man sat on the donkey, and the driver walked beside him, urging the animal forward whenever he didn't go fast enough.

But the day was hot, and towards noon the heat grew unbearable. They were in the middle of a stony desert without a tree or bush in sight. The young man said he could go no farther, so he got off the donkey and sat down in its shadow. But the driver had something to say about that.

"That's my place," he said. "Move over and let me sit there!"

"Certainly not," said the young man. "I hired this donkey for the whole journey, didn't I?"

"You hired the donkey, to be sure," agreed the driver. "But you didn't hire his shadow. That belongs to me!"

So the driver and the young man fell to arguing and quarrelling, and in the midst of their quarrel the donkey grew tired of standing still, took to his heels and made off as fast as he could go.

So both the young man and the driver were left in the middle of the desert with nothing but their own feet to get them out of it.

It doesn't always pay to argue.

The Donkey's Shadow

The Hare and the Tortoise

Hare and Tortoise

Tortoise was very little when his mother said to him, "You will never be able to go very fast. We Tortoises are a slow-moving family, but we get there in the end. Don't try to run. Remember, 'steady and slow' does it." Tortoise remembered these words.

One day when he was grown up, he was walking quietly round in a field minding his own business. Hare thought he would have some fun, so he ran round Tortoise in quick circles, just to annoy him. Hare was proud of himself because everyone knew he was one of the swiftest of animals. But Tortoise took no notice, so Hare stopped in front of him and laughed.

"Can't you move faster than that?" said Hare. "You'll never get anywhere at that rate! You should take a few lessons from me." Tortoise lifted his head slowly and said:

"I don't want to get anywhere, thank you. I've no need to go dashing about all over the place. You see, my thick shell protects me from my enemies."

"But how dull life must be for you!" Hare went on. "Why, it takes you half an hour to cross one field, while I can be away out of sight in half a minute. Besides, you really do look silly, you know! You ought to be ashamed of yourself."

Well, at this Tortoise was rather annoyed. Hare was really very provoking.

"Look here," said Tortoise, "if you want a race, I'll give you one; and I don't need any start either."

Hare laughed till the tears ran down his furry face, and his sides shook so much that he rolled over backwards. Tortoise just waited till Hare had finished, then he said:

"Well, what about it? I'm not joking."

Several other animals had gathered round, and they all said: "Go on, Hare. It's a challenge. You'll have to race him."

"Certainly," said Hare, "if you want to make a fool of yourself. Where shall we race to?"

Tortoise shaded his eyes with one foot and said:

"See that old windmill on the top of the hill yonder? We'll race to that. We can start from this tree-stump here. Come on, and may the best animal win!"

So as soon as they were both standing beside the tree-stump, Chanticleer the Cock shouted "Ready—steady—go!" and Tortoise began to crawl towards the far-off windmill. The other animals had hurried on ahead so as to see the finish.

Hare stood beside the tree-stump watching Tortoise waddle away across the field. The day was hot, and just beside the tree-stump was a pleasant, shady place, so he sat down and waited. He guessed it would take him about two and a half minutes to reach the windmill, even without trying very hard, so there was no hurry—no hurry at all. Presently he began to drop off to sleep. Two or three minutes passed, and Hare opened one eye lazily. Tortoise had scarcely crossed the first field. "Steady and slow," he said to himself under his breath. "Steady and slow. That's what mother said." And he kept on towards the far-off windmill.

"At that rate," said Hare to himself sleepily, "it'll take him just about two hours to get there—if he doesn't drop dead on the way."

He closed his eye again and fell into a deep sleep.

After a while Tortoise had crossed the first field, and was making his way slowly over the second.

"Steady and slow does it," he muttered to himself.

The sun began to go down, and at last Hare woke up, feeling chilly.

"Where am I?" he thought, "What's happened? Oh yes, I remember."

He got to his feet and looked towards the windmill. But where was Tortoise? He was nowhere to be seen. Hare jumped on to the tree-stump and strained his eyes to gaze into the distance. There, half-way across the very last field before the windmill, was a tiny black dot. Tortoise!

"This won't do," said Hare. "I must have overslept. I'd better be moving."

So he sprang from the stump and darted across the first field, then the second, then the third. It was really much farther than he had thought.

At the windmill the other animals were waiting to see the finish. At last Tortoise arrived, rather out of breath and wobbling a little on his legs.

"Come on, Tortoise!" they shouted.

Then Hare appeared at the far side of the last field, streaking along like the wind. How he ran! Not even Stag, when he was being hunted, could go faster. Even Swallow could scarcely fly faster through the blue sky.

"Steady and slow," said Tortoise to himself, but no one could hear him, for he had very, very little breath left to talk with.

"Come on, Tortoise!" cried some animals, and a few cried, "Come on, Hare! He's beating you!"

Hare put on extra speed and ran faster than he had ever run before. But it was no good. He had given Tortoise too much start, and he was still twenty yards behind when Tortoise crawled over the last foot of ground and tumbled up against the windmill. He had won the race!

All the animals cheered, and after that Hare never laughed at Tortoise again.

Slow and steady wins the race.

THE SICK LION

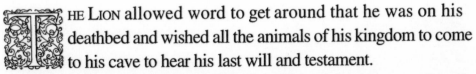HE LION allowed word to get around that he was on his deathbed and wished all the animals of his kingdom to come to his cave to hear his last will and testament.

Fox, who lived by his wits, did not wish to be the first to enter the cave. So he lingered near the entrance while Goat and Sheep and Calf went in to receive the last wishes of the King of Beasts.

After a time, Lion seemed to make a remarkable recovery, and came to the mouth of the cave. Seeing Fox a safe distance away, he bellowed: "Why do you not come in to pay your respects to me, friend Fox?"

"Please pardon me, your majesty," replied Fox, "but I do not wish to crowd you. I noticed the tracks of many of your subjects going into your cave, but so far I have seen none coming out. Until some of them come out, and there is more room in the cave, I think I'll stay out here in the open air."

Don't believe all you hear.

THE GOOSE WITH THE GOLDEN EGGS

THE FARMER WENT to the nest of his goose to see whether she had laid an egg. To his surprise he found, instead of an ordinary goose egg, an egg of solid gold. Seizing the golden egg he rushed to the house in great excitement to show it to his wife.

Every day thereafter the goose laid an egg of pure gold. But as the farmer grew rich he grew greedy. And thinking that if he killed the goose he could have all her treasure at once, he cut her open only to find—nothing at all.

The greedy who want more lose all.

MERCURY AND THE SCULPTOR

THERE WERE often times when Mercury, between errands on Olympus, yearned to know whether he still was held in high esteem by mankind.

So one day, disguising himself as a traveller, he visited a sculptor's studio. Walking about among the many statues displayed there, he pointed to an image or Jupiter.

"How much are you asking for this odd piece?" he asked.

"I'll let you have that one cheap," replied the sculptor. "It is one of our less popular numbers. One drachma."

Mercury laughed in his sleeve. Then he asked: "How much for this stout lady here?"

The sculptor said: "Oh, that one is Juno. I have to get a little more for females."

Mercury's eye now caught sight of an image of himself. Thinking that as Messenger of the Gods and source of all commercial gain his image would command a gratifying high price, he said: "I see you have a very handsome statue there of Mercury. How high do you value that excellent likeness?"

"Well," replied the sculptor, "I am willing to make you a bargain. If you will pay me the price I quoted to you on the other two statues, I will throw this one in free."

He who seeks a compliment
sometimes discovers the truth.

THE BLIND MAN AND THE CUB

HERE WAS ONCE a blind man who, merely by placing his hands upon an animal, could determine to what species it belonged. To test him one day they brought him a wolf's cub. Long and carefully he felt the beast all over. Then, still being in doubt, he said: "I know not whether thy father was a dog or a wolf, but this I do know, that I would not trust thee among a flock of sheep."

The child is father to the man.

THE FOX AND THE HEDGEHOG

FOX IN SOME unaccountable fashion got his tail entangled in a thicket which held him as closely as though he had been caught in a trap. In no time at all myriads of mosquitoes, seeing his plight, settled down upon him to enjoy a good meal undisturbed by his brush.

Hedgehog, who chanced to be strolling by felt sorry for Fox and approached him, saying: "Friend Fox, you seem to be in a most unfortunate situation. Would you like me to make you more comfortable by driving off these blood-sucking pests?"

But to Hedgehog's surprise Fox replied: "No; thank you, my good friend, but I beg you not to disturb them."

"And why not?" persisted the well-meaning Hedgehog.

"Well, you see," replied Fox, "these mosquitoes which you see have already drawn their fill of blood. If you chase them away a fresh swarm of hungry ones will descend upon me and they will not leave a drop of blood in my body."

A needy thief steals more
than one who enjoys plenty.

THE HAWK AND THE PIGEONS

A HAWK HAD LONG had his eye on a flock of pigeons, but no matter how often he had swooped down upon them from the sky they always had been able to reach their shelter in safety. Thinking that it might be his shadow they had spied, he waited for a cloudy day for his next attack, but still to no avail.

At length, hungry Hawk decided to use craft instead of attack. From the top of a near-by dead tree he called down to the pigeons: "Why do you prefer this life of constant fear and anxiety when, if you would make me your king, I could patrol the sky and make you safe from any attack that could be made upon you?"

The foolish pigeons, believing Hawk's interest in their welfare to be sincere, called him to the throne as their king and protector. But no sooner was he established there than he issued an order that every day one pigeon would have to be sacrificed for his dinner.

They who voluntarily put themselves under the power of a tyrant deserve whatever fate they receive.

THE DONKEY AND HIS DRIVER

A FARMER WAS driving a donkey along a country lane on the way to town. The beast bore no burden and was allowed to amble along at his own pace. Suddenly the idea came to him to leave the beaten track and make for the edge of a precipice which bordered the roadway.

When he was just on the point of falling over, his master ran up and, seizing him by the tail, tried with might and main to pull him back. Wilfully, Donkey resisted, pulling the opposite way. The farmer, seeing that he was about to be pulled over the precipice along with the stubborn beast, let go his hold. As Donkey went hurtling over the brink his master cried after him: "Well, Jack, if you will be master, you will have to continue on alone."

A wilful beast must go his own way.

JUPITER, NEPTUNE, MINERVA AND MOMUS

AGES AND ages ago, when the world was young, Jupiter, Neptune, and Minerva used to spend a great deal of time disputing as to which could make the most perfect thing. So it was decided that they would have a contest with Momus (at that time he had not yet been turned out of Olympus) to decide which creation had the greatest merit.

Jupiter made a man. Neptune made a bull. Minerva made a house. Then Judge Momus came to judge the contest. He began by finding fault with Neptune's bull because his horns were not below his eyes so that he could see when he gored with them. Next he found fault with the man because there was no window in his breast in order that all might see his inward thoughts and feelings. And lastly, he found fault with the house because it had no wheels to enable its inhabitants to move away from bad neighbours.

Jupiter, incensed with the carping critic who could not be pleased, forthwith drove the fault-finding judge out of the home of the gods.

It is time to criticize the works of others
when you have done some good thing yourself.

THE HARE WITH MANY FRIENDS

THERE WAS once a hare who had so many friends in the forest and the field she truly felt herself to be the most popular member of the animal kingdom. One day she heard the hounds approaching.

"Why should a popular creature like me have to run for her life every time she hears a dog?" said she to herself. So she went to the horse, and asked him to carry her away from the hounds on his back.

"There is nothing I would rather do, friend Hare," said Horse, "but, unfortunately, right now I have some important work to do for my master. However, a popular creature like you should have no difficulty in getting someone to help you."

Then Hare went to Bull and asked him whether he would be kind enough to ward off the hounds with his horns.

"My dear friend," replied the Bull, "you know how I feel about you, and how glad I always am to be of service. But at this very moment I have an appointment with a lady. Why don't you ask our mutual friend Goat?"

But Goat was busy too, and so was Ram, and so were Calf and Pig and Ass. Each assured Hare of his undying friendship and anxiety to aid her in her trouble, but each had some excuse which prevented him from performing the service. By this time the hounds were quite near, so the hare took to her heels and luckily escaped .

He who has many friends has no friends.

THE DONKEY EATING THISTLES

AT HARVEST time the master and the reapers were out in the field. When the sun was high in the sky the maidservants loaded the Donkey with good things to eat and drink and sent him to the field. On his way he noticed a fine large thistle growing in the lane, and being hungry he began to eat it. As he chewed it slowly, he reflected: "How many greedy people would think themselves happy amidst such a variety of delicacies as I am carrying. But for my taste, this bitter, prickly thistle is more savoury and appetizing than the most sumptuous banquet."

One man's meat may be another man's poison.

THE FARMER AND HIS DOGS

THE WINTER WAS the coldest within the memory of the oldest living inhabitant. The roads were blocked by snowdrifts so deep that people could not struggle through them. A farmer found himself completely isolated with the drifts piled up to the eaves of his house. When his provisions ran out he was forced to slaughter one of his own sheep for food. Still the bitter weather continued. When all his sheep had been consumed he was forced to eat up his goats. And at last for there still was no break in the terrible winter— the farmer had to sacrifice his valuable plough oxen to keep his family from starving.

When the dogs observed that the cattle had gone the same way as the sheep and goats they said to one another: "Let us be off, no matter how deep the snow. For if our master had had no pity on the working oxen, how is it likely then that he will spare us?"

When our neighbours house is on fire,
it is time to look to our own.

LION AND MOUSE

THE DAY WAS very hot, and Lion was sleeping under a rock. He was a big lion, very splendid and noble; in fact, as everyone knows, he was King of All Animals. Now it so happened that Mouse had lost her way. Running hither and thither, she stumbled over Lion's very nose and woke him. Instantly Lion put out a paw and held Mouse fast to the ground. Mice, as everyone knows, are very little animals, and this mouse was specially little. But she stuck her head out from under Lion's paw and began to squeak piteously.

"Oh, Your Majesty," she squeaked, "please forgive me. I didn't mean to trip over Your Majesty's nose and wake Your Majesty, truly I didn't. Of course Your Majesty *could* squash me dead with one squash, but would it be worth it for such a noble and dignified animal as a lion to squash such a miserable little creature as a mouse?"

"Stop squeaking!" ordered Lion. "Tell me why should I be merciful to such an insignificant creature as you."

"Well," said Mouse, "it is a noble act for a King to be merciful. It shows how noble he is. Besides, Your Majesty, perhaps one day even a miserable little creature like me *might* be able to do Your Majesty a good turn. Who knows?"

"Ho, ho, ho!" laughed Lion, King of All Animals, with a great roar that nearly terrified Mouse out of her small wits. "That's a good one— a mouse help a lion! Well, that's a good joke, upon my whiskers."

And he twiddled his whiskers to show what fine whiskers they were, and also how amused he was.

The Lion and the Mouse

"Well, I didn't say it *would* happen," said Mouse, "I only said it might."

And *she* twiddled *her* whiskers, just to show that she too had whiskers, even though they were such little whiskers .

"Very well," said Lion. "Off you go, and leave me to my sleep. And in future mind where you're going."

"Oh I will, Your Majesty," said Mouse. "Thank you so very much for sparing my life."

But Lion only snored. He was asleep again.

Well, a long time afterwards, Lion was roaming through the jungle, not looking where he was going, because he was King of All Animals and had become just a bit careless, so he fell right into a trap that some hunters had set for him. It was a deep pit covered over with a net hidden by leaves. Into the pit fell Lion with the net all round him, so that he got tangled up in it and couldn't free himself. So he let out a great roar, and the whole jungle shook with his roaring, and every creature in the jungle trembled with fear.

Not far off the little mouse put down a corn-stalk she was nibbling and said to herself: "Now where have I heard *that* noise before? Why, of course, it's King Lion, and it sounds as if he's in trouble."

So in less than one minute she had run to the place where Lion was caught in the net, and began to bite through the strings of the net. Soon she had made a hole large enough for Lion to get through, so he was able to escape and wasn't caught by the hunters after all. I am sorry to say that he didn't thank Mouse quite as graciously as he ought to have done. But Mouse did not mind. She scampered away to look for the corn-stalk she had put down when she heard King Lion's roar.

Kindness is never thrown away—no one is so unimportant that he may not be able to repay a good turn.

THE THIEF AND THE DOG

A THIEF was clambering over the wall when the Watchdog began barking.

"Be still," hissed the thief, "I am one of your master's friends."

But the Dog kept on growling and barking. Hoping to silence him, the thief reached into a bag and tossed some scraps of food down to the Dog.

"No, you don't," snapped the Watchdog. "I had my suspicions of you before, but now that you are so free with your gifts I am sure your intentions are evil."

A bribe in hand betrays mischief at heart.

THE TRAVELLERS AND THE HATCHET

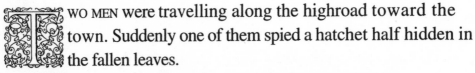WO MEN were travelling along the highroad toward the town. Suddenly one of them spied a hatchet half hidden in the fallen leaves.

"Look what I have found!" he cried, picking up the tool.

"Do not say *'I,'*" replied his companion. "It is more proper to say, 'Look what *we* have found!'"

The finder of the hatchet shrugged his shoulders, and they continued on their way. Presently they came upon a group of men whose eyes were on the roadway as though they were looking for something. Suddenly one of the strangers pointed to the approaching twain, and they rushed up to them, pointing to the hatchet.

"Alas," said the traveller who had found the hatchet, "it looks as though we are in trouble."

"What do you mean *'we* are in trouble'? What you really mean to say is that 'I am in trouble!'"

He who will not allow his friend to share the prize
must not expect him to share the danger.

The Lion and the Dolphin

THE KING of Beasts was pacing majestically along the shore of the sea one day when he spied a dolphin basking on the surface of the water.

"Hello, there, friend Dolphin!" roared Lion. "This is a fortunate meeting, indeed. I long have wanted to suggest that you and I form an alliance. As I am the King of the Beasts and you are the King of the Fishes, what is more natural than that we should be strong friends and powerful allies?"

"There is much in what you say," replied Dolphin.

Not long afterward Lion again came to the seashore where he was challenged by a wild bull. The fight was not going too well for Lion, so he called upon Dolphin for his promised support. The latter, though ready and willing to aid his ally, found himself unable to come out of the sea to join the battle. After the Wild Bull had been put to flight, Lion rebuked the dolphin.

"You are a fine ally," said Lion. "I could have been killed, and you never turned a fin to help me."

"Do not blame me," said Dolphin in reply, "but blame nature, which made me powerful in the sea but altogether helpless on land."

*In choosing allies look to their power
as well as their will to help you.*

The Boy Bathing

A BOY WAS walking by the bank of the river on a warm day in spring. He could not resist the temptation to remove his clothes and plunge in for the first swim of the year. But the water proved to be much colder and deeper than it had appeared from the shore. The boy was on the point of sinking when he caught sight of a wayfarer strolling along the shore.

"Help! Help!" screamed the boy. "I am drowning. Save me!"

Instead of plunging in at once to the lad's rescue, the traveller called out: "You foolish young man, don't you realize that this is not the season to go bathing? What would your mother say if she knew you were in the river at this time of year? I have a good mind to report this matter to the authorities. Whatever were you thinking of—"

"Oh, save me now, sir," interrupted the struggling boy, "and read me the lecture afterward!"

There is a time and place for everything.

The Boasting Traveller

A YOUNG man who had been travelling in foreign parts returned to his home city where he bragged and boasted to all who would listen of the great feats he had accomplished in the places he had visited.

"Why, when I was in Rhodes," he shouted, thumping his chest, "I made the most extraordinary leap the people of that place ever had seen. I have witnesses to prove it, too."

In time his listeners became weary of the traveller's boasts, and one of them said: "These exploits of yours in Rhodes may all be true, but you can save yourself much breath by doing one of those marvellous leaps right now instead of merely talking about it."

He who does a thing well does not need to boast.

THE EAGLE AND THE ARROW

A BOWMAN saw an eagle soaring lazily in the sky one day. Quickly he notched an arrow and sent it whizzing after the bird. It found its mark, and the Eagle felt itself wounded to death. As it slowly fluttered down to earth it saw that the half of the arrow which had pierced its breast was fitted with one of its own feathers.

How often do we supply our enemies
with the means of our own destruction!

The Farmer and the Nightingale

AFTER A HARD DAY'S work a farmer went early to bed. But he could not go to sleep because of the melodious singing of a nightingale all through the summer night. So pleased was he by the bird's song that the next night he set a trap for it and captured it.

"Ah, my beauty," said he, "now that I have caught you, you shall hang in a cage and sing for me every night."

"But we nightingales never sing in a cage," replied Nightingale. "If you imprison me I shall sicken and die and you shall never hear my song again."

"Then I'll put you in a pie and eat you," said the farmer. "I always have heard that nightingale pie is a dainty morsel."

"Please do not kill me," begged Nightingale. "If you will set me free I'll tell you three great truths that will be worth far more to you than my poor body."

So the farmer set him loose, and he flew up to a branch of a tree.

"Hold on," said the farmer, "what are the three great truths you promised me?"

Nightingale trilled a few happy notes and said: "Never believe a captive's promise. Keep what you have. And never sorrow over what is lost forever." Then the songbird flew away.

A bird in the cage is worth two on a branch.

THE FOX AND THE WOODMAN

HE FOX, HARD pressed by a pack of hounds who had been chasing him over hill and dale, came up to a man who was cutting wood outside his cottage.

"Please, kind sir," panted the weary Fox, "will you hide me in a corner where I will be safe from the hunters' hounds who wish to kill me?"

The man showed him his own hut, and Fox, creeping in, hid himself in a corner. Presently the hunters came up.

"Have you seen a fox hereabouts?" they asked.

"Why, no," replied the woodman. "I have been chopping wood here all morning." As he spoke he pointed with his finger to the very corner of the cottage where the fox was hiding. The hunters, not knowing what he meant, called their dogs and rode away.

As soon as the danger was past the fox sneaked out of his hiding place and would have departed without a word of thanks.

"Just a moment, there, friend Fox," the woodman said. "Is this the way you take leave of your host, without even a thank you for saving your life?"

"A pretty host!" snapped Fox. "If you had been as honest with your finger as you were with your tongue, then I should not have left your roof without bidding you farewell."

There is as much malice in a wink as in a word.

The Gardener and his Dog

HE GARDENER was drawing water at the well to water his garden plants. His little dog was jumping and barking on the well edge until he lost his balance and fell in.

Hearing the splash, the gardener quickly drew off his clothes and descended into the well to rescue his dog. Just as he was bringing the struggling and slippery animal to the top, the ungrateful wretch bit his master's hand.

"Why, you little monster," exclaimed the gardener. "If that is your idea of gratitude to a master who feeds you and pets you and treats you kindly, then pull yourself out of the well." With that he dropped the dog right back into the well again.

Don't bite the hand that feeds you!

THE DONKEY AND THE LAP DOG

A DONKEY AND a lap dog belonged to the same master. Tied up in the stable the Donkey had plenty of corn and hay to eat, and he should have been more than contented with his lot, even though he was kept busy hauling wood all day, and on occasion had to take his turn at the mill at night.

Meanwhile the little dog was always sporting and gambling about, caressing and fawning upon his master to such an extent that he became a great favourite and was permitted to lie in his master's lap. Needless to say, Donkey began to feel sorry for himself. It galled him to see the Lap Dog living in such ease and luxury, enjoying the favour of the master.

Thinking that if he behaved in the same fashion toward his master he would fare the same, one day he broke from his halter and rushed into the house where his owner was having his dinner. Here he pranced about, swishing his tail and imitating as best he could the frolics of the Lap Dog, finally upsetting the dinner table and smashing all the crockery. Nor did he stop there. He jumped upon his master and pawed him with his roughshod feet.

At length the servants, seeing their master in no little danger, released him from Donkey's wild caresses. Thereupon they so belaboured the silly creature with sticks and stones that he never got up again.

To be satisfied with one's lot is better than to desire
something which one is not fitted to receive.

The Falconer and the Partridge

A FALCONER discovered that he had captured a partridge in his net. The bird cried out piteously when he approached: "Please, Master Falconer, let me go. If you will set me free I promise you that I will decoy other partridges into your net."

"No," replied the falconer. "I might have set you free. But one who is ready to betray his innocent friends to save his own miserable life deserves, if possible, a fate worse than death."

Treachery is the basest crime of all.

THE EAGLE, WILDCAT AND SOW

AN EAGLE chose the top branches of an old oak tree for her nest and hatched her young there. A wildcat had selected the hollow trunk of the same tree for her den where she would raise her little ones. And down among the roots of the old oak a sow had burrowed a hole where she planned to raise her piglets in comfort.

For some time all three families lived peacefully in the old oak, until Wildcat took the notion to start gossiping about her neighbours.

"Neighbour," she whispered to Eagle, "as you know I have the highest respect for Old Sow down below. But if she keeps rooting under this tree the whole thing will come crashing down someday. That's probably what she has in mind so she can feed our babies to her litter."

Needless to say, Mother Eagle was worried. She was so disturbed that she did not dare to leave her nest to go in search of food. Meanwhile, the gossiping Wildcat visited the Sow.

"Mrs. Sow," she whispered, "I'm no gossip, as you know, but if I were you I wouldn't leave home today. I overheard that Eagle upstairs telling her children they were going to have pork for supper."

So Eagle stayed in her nest and Sow remained with her little pigs. But Wildcat sneaked off every night and got all the food for her kittens, while her neighbours lived in distrust of each other.

It is possible that both families would have starved to death had not the Wildcat made the mistake of getting caught in a hunter's snare, and Sow and Eagle became reunited in caring for the abandoned kittens.

Gossips are to be seen and not heard.

The Frogs Desiring a King

HE Frogs had always lived a happy life in the marshes. They had jumped and splashed about with never a care in the world. Yet some of them were not satisfied with their easygoing life. They thought they should have a king to rule over them and to watch over their morals. So they decided to send a petition to Jupiter asking him to appoint a king.

Jupiter was amused by the Frogs' plea. Good-naturedly he threw down a log into the lake, which landed with such a splash that it sent all the Frogs scampering for safety. But after a while, when one venturesome Frog saw that the log lay still, he encouraged his friends to approach the fallen monster. In no time at all the Frogs, growing bolder and bolder, swarmed over the log Jupiter had sent and treated it with the greatest contempt.

Dissatisfied with so tame a ruler, they petitioned Jupiter a second time, saying: "We want a real king, a king who will really rule over us." Jupiter, by this time, had lost some of his good nature and was tired of the Frogs' complaining.

So he sent them the Stork, who proceeded to gobble up the Frogs right and left. After a few days the survivors sent Mercury with a private message to Jupiter, beseeching him to take pity on them once more.

"Tell them." said Jupiter coldly, "that this is their own doing. They wanted a king. They will have to make the best of what they asked for."

Let well enough alone!

The Donkey and the Grasshopper

A DONKEY heard some Grasshoppers chirping and singing merrily on a fine summer day. Delighted with the music, and hoping to learn the secret of their musical ability, the Donkey approached them.

"My fine fellows," said he, "upon what do you feed that makes you sing so sweetly all day long?"

When the Grasshoppers told the foolish Donkey that they supped upon nothing but dew, he galloped off determined to exist upon the same diet. In time he died of hunger.

Even a fool is wise—when it is too late!

THE MICE IN THE COUNCIL

FOR MANY years the Mice had been living in constant dread of their enemy, the Cat. It was decided to call a meeting to determine the best means of handling the situation. Many plans were discussed and rejected.

At last a young mouse got up. "I propose," said he, looking very important, "that a bell be hung around Cat's neck. Then whenever Cat approaches, we always shall have notice of her presence, and so be able to escape."

The young Mouse sat down amidst tremendous applause. The suggestion was put to a motion and passed almost unanimously .

But just then an old Mouse, who had sat silent all the while, rose to his feet and said: "My friends, it takes a young mouse to think of a plan so ingenious and yet so simple. With a bell about Cat's neck to warn us we shall all be safe. I have but one brief question to put to the supporters of the plan—which one of you is going to put the bell on the Cat?"

It is one thing to propose, another to execute.

THE FOX WITHOUT A TAIL

THE Fox had the misfortune to have his bushy tail caught in a trap. When he saw that it was a question of his life or his tail he left his tail behind him. He felt himself disgraced, however, and for a time did not go near his friends for fear of ridicule.

But one day the idea came to him how he could make the best of a bad bargain. He called a meeting of all the rest of the Foxes and proposed to them that they should follow his example.

"You have no idea," said he, "of the ease and comfort I am enjoying. I don't know why I didn't cut off my tail long ago. I could never have believed it if I had not tried it myself. When you come to think about it, friends, a tail is such an inconvenient and unnecessary appendage that it is strange we have put up with it so long. My sincere advice to you all is to share this new freedom and part with your tails at once."

As he concluded, one of the older and wiser Foxes stepped forward and said: "There is not one of us who does not believe that you found it convenient to cut off your tail. However, we are not so convinced that you would advise us to part with our tails if there were any chance of recovering your own."

Misery loves company.

THE EAGLE AND THE CROW

N EAGLE swooped down from a high rock and pounced upon a lamb, grazing near her mother in the field. With a great beating of powerful wings he seized the Lamb and flew away to his nest.

Crow sat in an oak tree watching Eagle's exploit. Said he to himself: "Surely that is an easy way to find oneself a dinner." So, spying the sturdy old Ram below him, he bore down with all the force he could muster, intending to carry the Ram off as a prize. He fastened his claws in the wool and tugged with all his might. But nothing happened. As a matter of fact, the Ram wouldn't have known he was there if it had not been for Crow's frantic efforts to disentangle his claws from the wool.

Crow's squawking attracted the attention of the shepherd, who came up and caught him and clipped his wings and took him home to the children for a pet.

It requires more than wings to be an eagle.

The Raven and the Swan

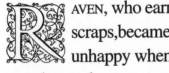AVEN, who earned a comfortable livelihood picking up scraps, became dissatisfied with his lot. He was especially unhappy whenever he saw Swan floating gracefully about a nearby pool.

"What makes that swan so white and beautiful?" he would say. "Could it be that the water has magic qualities to turn one's feathers from black to white?"

So Raven left his comfortable home and went to the pools and streams. There he washed and plumed his feathers, but all to no purpose. His plumage remained as black as ever, and before long he perished for want of his usual perch.

A change of scene does not change one's character.

THE FARMER AND THE STORK

A FARMER, who was tired of having his newly planted corn stolen by the Cranes, set a net in his field. When he went to examine his snare he found that he had caught several of them, and included in their number was a Stork.

"Please, sir," begged Stork, "don't kill me. I am not one of these greedy Cranes who eat all your corn. I am a good and pious bird. I take care of my aged parents. I—"

But the farmer cut him short. "All that you say about yourself may be true. All I know, however, is that I have caught you with those who were destroying my crops, and I'm afraid that you will have to suffer the same fate as those in whose company you were captured."

You are judged by the company you keep.

THE HARE AND THE HOUND

A HOUND, WHILST out hunting by himself, flushed a hare from a thicket and gave chase. The frightened Hare gave the Dog a long run and escaped. As the disappointed Hound turned back toward home, a passing goat-herd said jeeringly: "You are a fine hunter! Aren't you ashamed to let a little Hare one-tenth your size get the better of you?"

"You forget," replied the Hound, "that I was only running for my supper, but the Hare was running for his life!"

Necessity is our strongest weapon.

THE EAGLE AND THE BEETLE

A HARE, PURSUED by an eagle, sought refuge in the nest of a beetle. Hare asked Beetle to save him. Beetle interceded with Eagle and begged him to leave hare alone. But Eagle in his wrath gave Beetle a flop with his wing and immediately seized upon the Hare and devoured him.

When Eagle flew away, Beetle flew after him in order to learn where his nest was hidden. Then one day when Eagle was away, Beetle returned and rolled Eagle's eggs out of the nest, one by one, and broke them. Grieved and enraged that anyone should attempt so audacious a thing, Eagle built his nest in a higher place. But again his eggs suffered a similar fate.

In desperation Eagle flew up to Jupiter, his lord and king, and placed the third brood of eggs, as a sacred deposit, in his lap, begging him to guard them from harm. But Beetle, having made a little ball of dirt, flew up with it and dropped it in Jupiter's lap. The god, rising quickly to shake it off, and forgetting the eggs, dropped them and they were broken.

Jupiter, knowing that Beetle was in the right, but loath to see the race of Eagles diminished, used his good offices to persuade Beetle to call a truce with Eagle. This Beetle would not agree to do, and Jupiter was forced to transfer Eagle's breeding to another season, when there were no Beetles to be seen.

The laws of hospitality are not to be broken with impunity.

THE FROG AND THE OX

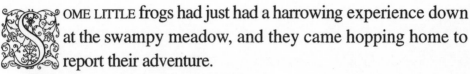

Some little frogs had just had a harrowing experience down at the swampy meadow, and they came hopping home to report their adventure.

"Oh, father," said one of the little frogs, all out of breath, "we have just seen the most terrible monster in all the world. It was enormous, with horns on its head and a long tail and hoofs—"

"Why, child, that was no monster. That was only Ox. He isn't so big! If I really put my mind to it I could make myself as big as Ox. Just watch me!" So Old Frog blew himself up. "Was he as big as I am now?" he asked.

"Oh, father, much bigger," cried the little frogs. Again the father frog blew himself up, and asked his children if Ox could be as big as that.

"Bigger, father, a great deal bigger," came the chorus from the little frogs. "If you blew yourself up until you burst you could not be as big as the monster we saw in the swampy meadow."

Provoked by such disparagement of his powers, Old Frog made one more attempt. He blew and blew and swelled and swelled until something went *pop*. Old Frog had burst.

Self-conceit leads to self-destruction.

THE HORSE AND THE GROOM

THERE WAS once a groom who was just about the meanest man in the world. He used to steal the grain intended for the horses and, without his master's knowledge, sell it in the village. But all day long he kept very busy rubbing down and grooming the Horse within an inch of his life.

"If you really are so anxious that I look well," said Horse one day to his groom, "then give me less of your brushing and more of your corn."

A *man may smile, yet be a villain.*

THE LION, THE BEAR AND THE FOX

A LION AND A BEAR found the carcass of a fawn. Both were hungry. Both wanted it. So they started to fight for it. The contest was long and hard and savage. At last, when both of them, half blinded and half dead, lay panting on the ground without the strength to touch the prize before them, Fox came by.

Noting the helpless condition of the two beasts, the impudent Fox stepped nimbly between them, seized the fawn over which they had battled, and with never a "thank you" dragged it away to his den.

*Only fools fight to exhaustion while a rogue
runs off with the dinner.*

THE FARTHING RUSHLIGHT

A LONG TIME ago people lighted their homes with candles made of the pith of rushes dipped in grease. These candles were known as rushlights. There was one particular rushlight which had soaked up considerable grease and was feeling more than a little boastful.

One evening it announced before a large company that it could outshine the sun, the moon, and the stars. At that very moment a puff of wind came and blew it out. The servant who relighted it said: "Shine on, friend rushlight, and hold your tongue, there is no wind strong enough to blow out the lights of heaven."

Know thy place and keep it.

THE HAWK AND THE FARMER

A PRUDENT FARMER had spread a net over his corn-field to catch the crows who liked to dig up his newly planted seeds. One day Hawk, pursuing a pigeon, flew so swiftly over the farmer's corn-field that before he knew it he found himself caught in the snare.

The farmer, observing Hawk struggling in the net, went over to the captured bird of prey.

"This is all a mistake," said Hawk as the farmer approached. "I was just chasing a pigeon, and the wretched bird flew right over your field. I was not going to do a bit of harm to you. Believe me, sir!"

"That may be," replied the farmer. "But unless you can tell me just what harm the pigeon had done to you, I'm afraid I'm going to have to wring your neck."

Hypocrisy is the cloak of villainy.

The Bull and the Goat

A BULL, PURSUED by a lion, took shelter in a cave which was the home of a wild goat. Greatly annoyed with the intruder, Goat began to butt the tired Bull with his horns. He bore the ill-treatment of Goat with patience, saying: "Because I permit you to vent your displeasure on me now, does not mean that I am afraid of you. As soon as Lion is out of sight and the danger is past, then I will show you the difference between Lion and Goat."

Those who take temporary advantage of their neighbours difficulties may live to repent of their insolence.

THE HORSE AND THE LADEN DONKEY

THERE WAS once a man who kept a horse and a donkey as beasts of burden. It was his custom to load Donkey until he could barely stagger under the weight, while Horse was allowed to prance along in its fine trappings with a very light load.

As they were proceeding along the road one day, Donkey, who had been ailing for the past several days, said to Horse: "Will you relieve me of part of my load for a few miles? I feel dreadfully unwell, but if you will carry a fair portion of the freight today I shall soon get well again. This weight is killing me."

Horse, however, merely kicked up his heels and told the donkey not to trouble him with his complaints. Donkey staggered along for another half mile in silence, then suddenly fell to the ground dead.

Just then the master came up, and perceiving what had happened, he removed the load from the dead donkey and placed it on Horse's back. "Alas," groaned the horse, as he started off with the heavy load augmented by Donkey's carcass, "now am I rewarded for my ill-nature. By refusing to bear my fair share of the load, I now must carry the whole of it plus the dead weight of my poor companion."

A bad temper carries with it its own punishment.

THE HEDGE AND THE VINEYARD

FOOLISH young heir came into the possession of his wise father's estate. After the funeral and when his inheritance was securely in his hands, the young man ordered his servants to cut down all of the hedges that surrounded his vineyard. When the servants sought to dissuade their new master from his purpose he shouted: "Why should they not be torn down? They bear no grapes; they yield no harvest; they occupy good land that should be planted to vines.Pull them up and burn them."

So the fences were torn down and the vineyard was open to the ravages of man and beast, and it was not long before the vines were all destroyed. And thus the simple fellow learned, when it was too late, that while it is true that one ought not to expect to gather grapes from brambles, yet it is quite as important to protect one's vineyard as to possess it.

They also serve who only stand and wait.

The Dog and Dog's Reflection

The Fox and the Grapes

THE LION AND THE BULLS

HE LION often prowled about a pasture where three bulls grazed together. He had tried without success to lure one or the other of them to the edge of the pasture. He had even attempted a direct attack, only to see them form a ring so that from whatever direction he approached he was met by the horns of one of them.

Then a plan began to form in Lion's mind. Secretly he started spreading evil and slanderous reports of one bull against the other. The three bulls, distrustingly, began to avoid one another, and each withdrew to a different part of the pasture to graze. of course, this was exactly what Lion wanted. One by one he fell upon the bulls, and so made easy prey of them all.

United we stand; divided we fall.

The Kid and the Wolf

HERE WAS once a very active kid who would leave the other goats in the farmyard below and climb onto the steep roof of the farmhouse.

"Look at me, mother," he would call down. "You are afraid to come up here where I am." The other goats paid very little attention to the boasting Kid, but one day Wolf passed by the farmhouse. He gave one look at Kid on the rooftop and would have passed by since it was easy to see that here was one dinner that was safely out of his reach. But Kid jeered and bleated: "Why don't you try to come up and catch me, coward?"

Wolf stopped, looked up again, and called back: "It is not you who call me coward, but the place on which you are standing."

If you must revile your neighbour,
make certain first that he cannot reach you.

THE MULE

MULE HAD been having an easy time of it with nothing to do but eat. One day as he was frisking about the pasture he began to fancy himself as a runner.

"My mother was a famous race horse. I'll bet I can run as fast as ever she could," he said to himself. And to prove it he set off at what he thought was a fast pace toward the barn.

Not so long afterward Mule's master found it necessary to get to the village in a great hurry. Jumping upon the animal's back the farmer began to whip him and urge him to greater speed, until Mule, gasping for breath said: "My mother may have been a race horse, but my father was only a jackass."

Every truth has two sides.

THE LION AND OTHER BEASTS
GO HUNTING

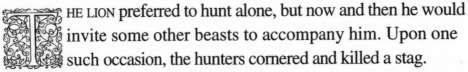

HE LION preferred to hunt alone, but now and then he would invite some other beasts to accompany him. Upon one such occasion, the hunters cornered and killed a stag.

Taking a commanding position before the dead stag, Lion roared: "Beasts, it is time to divide the spoils. I demand that it be quartered. The first quarter shall fall to me as King of the Beasts. The second is mine as arbiter. A third quarter is due me for my part in the chase. Now, as for the fourth part—" and here Lion gave an ominous growl "Let him take it who dares!"

Many may share in the labours but not in the spoils.

THE MAN AND THE SATYR

A MAN AND a satyr met on a woodland path, and as they journeyed along they struck up an acquaintance. The day was wintery and cold, and while they sat resting on a log the man put his fingers to his mouth and blew on them.

"What's that for, my friend?" asked the satyr.

"Oh, I always do that," replied the man, "when my hands are cold. I blow on them to warm them."

Shortly afterward they arrived at the satyr's home, and, he invited his companion in for a bowl of hot porridge. As the host placed a steaming bowl before his guest, the man raised his spoon to his lips and began blowing on it.

"And now what are you doing?" asked the satyr.

"Oh, my porridge is too hot to swallow, so I am blowing on it to cool it off," replied the man. And he went on blowing while the satyr stared in amazement.

Some men can blow hot and blow cold
with the same breath.

THE DONKEY AND HIS MASTERS

A DISCONTENTED donkey who felt that the gardener for whom he worked was a hard taskmaster appealed to Jupiter to give him another master. Annoyed by Donkey's ingratitude, Jupiter handed him over to a potter who gave him even heavier burdens to bear.

Again, Donkey appealed to Jupiter. This time it was arranged to have him sold to a tanner. Finding that he had fallen into worse hands than ever, Donkey said with a groan: "Alas, wretch that I am. Would that I had remained content with my former masters. My new owner not only works me harder while I am alive, but will not even spare my hide when I am dead!"

He that finds discontentment in one place is not likely to
find happiness in another.

The Nurse and the Wolf

"S TOP CRYING this instant," said an old nurse to the child who sat screaming on her lap, "or I will throw you out the window to the wolf."

At that very moment Wolf happened to be passing under the window and heard what the nurse had said. So he sat down to wait, saying to himself: "This must be my lucky day. From the way that baby is crying, my dinner ought to be coming out that window any minute now."

He waited and he waited. The baby stopped crying and went to sleep, and nothing happened. All through the cold night Wolf sat there, his mouth watering whenever he thought of the dainty morsel. He was tired and stiff from sitting in one position. Then, toward morning, the glad sound of a baby crying came from the window again.

Rushing to the window he looked up at the nurse and wagged his tail. But all the old nurse did was to shut the window with a bang and set the dogs upon the hungry wolf.

As he trotted away Wolf said to himself: "Next time I won't believe all I hear."

Enemies' promises are made to be broken.

The Two Crabs

A MOTHER crab and her child were strolling along the beach one day. It was a fine morning, but Mother Crab was too busy scolding her offspring to pay any attention to the weather.

"Why in the world, child, do you not walk as the other creatures do—forward instead of backward?" she complained.

"Mother, dear," replied the little crab, "do but set the example, yourself, and I will follow you."

Example is the best precept.

The Trumpeter Taken Prisoner

A TRUMPETER very rashly ventured too near the enemy, during a battle, and was taken prisoner.

"Spare me, good sirs, I beseech you," he begged of his captors. "Do not put me to death. I do not fight. I have never taken a life. I do not even carry a weapon, except this harmless trumpet, which I blow now and then."

"All the more reason you should die," replied the captors. "While you, yourself, have not the spirit to fight, you stir up the others to do battle and to take the lives of our comrades."

He who incites to strife is worse than he who takes part in it.

THE ONE-EYED DOE

A DOE WHO had had the misfortune to lose the sight of one of her eyes, and so could not see anyone approaching on that side, made it her practice to graze on a high cliff near the sea. Thus she kept her good eye toward the land on the lookout for hunters, while her blind side was toward the sea from where she feared no danger.

But one day some sailors were rowing past in a boat. Catching sight of the doe as she was grazing peacefully along the edge of the cliff, one of the sailors drew his bow and shot her. With her last gasp the dying doe said: "Alas, ill-fated creature that I am! I was safe on the land side, where I looked for danger, but my enemy came from the sea, to which I looked for protection."

Trouble comes from the direction we least expect it.

THE TWO POTS

WO POTS, one of earthenware and the other of brass, were carried downstream by a river in flood. The brass pot begged his companion to remain as close by his side as possible, and he would protect him.

"You are very kind," replied the earthenware pot, "but that is just what I am afraid of. If you will only keep your distance, I shall be able to float down in safety. But should we come too close, whether I strike you or your strike me, I am sure to be the one who will get the worst of it."

Avoid too powerful neighbours.

The Thief and the Boy

A BOY WAS playing by the edge of a well when a thief came walking by. Suddenly the boy began to cry. His little shoulders heaved with his sobbing. His wailing could be heard for a mile or more. When his grief had abated somewhat the thief said: "Why all the tears, my little friend?"

"Oh, dear, oh, dear," whimpered the boy. "I was playing with my beautiful silver mug. B-b-but the string broke and it fell down the well."

"That's easy," replied the thief. Tossing off his clothes he let himself down into the well. It was his intention to recover the valuable mug and keep it for himself.

Down, down, down he went. Colder and colder grew the water, but he couldn't find the mug—for the simple reason that there wasn't any! After a while the thief began to realize that the boy, having recognized him for a thief, had sent him down into the well to get him out of the way.

Painfully he climbed out of the well, shivering with the cold. When he reached the top again both the boy and the thief's clothes were gone.

He who tries to outsmart his neighbour
winds up by outsmarting himself.

THE THIEF AND HIS MOTHER

A SCHOOLBOY STOLE a book from one of his classmates and brought it home to his mother. Instead of chastising him, she said: "That was very clever of you, my son." As the boy grew older he began to steal things of greater value, until at length, being caught in the very act, he was arrested, tried, found guilty, and sentenced to be hanged.

The day of his execution arrived, and he was taken from his cell and led to the gallows. In the crowd that followed the cart the thief saw his mother, weeping and beating her breast. He begged the officers to be allowed to speak one word in his sorrowing mother's ear.

When she came near and inclined her head to hear his last words he suddenly bared his teeth and bit her savagely in the lobe of her ear. All the bystanders were horrified and pushed forward with threatening gestures toward the thief. They could not understand the inhuman conduct of a son toward his mother.

Then he cried out: "You think me a brute, and I am. But I have this woman to thank for the fact that I shall soon be swinging on the gallows. She is my mother. But when I was small and did mischief, instead of punishing me, she encouraged me to my ruin. Behold an unnatural son, because when I was small I had an unnatural mother."

Spare the rod and spoil the child.

THE STAG IN THE OX STALL

A STAG CLOSELY pursued by a pack of hounds sought refuge in the stable of a farmer. Trembling with fear he entered an empty ox stall where he tried to conceal himself under the straw. Only the stag's horns remained in sight. But the stable was dark, and when the hunters came along and asked whether anyone had seen the stag the stableboys looked, but could see nothing.

Stag began to take courage because he had not been discovered and thought that with the coming of darkness he would be able to make his escape.

"Don't be too sure," said Ox, from an adjoining stall. "When the master has finished his supper he will come to see that all is safe for the night. And then I fear that your life will be in jeopardy, for the master has eyes in the back of his head."

Even as he spoke, the farmer entered the stable. Pointing to the mound of straw, he called to the stableboys: "What are these two curious things sticking up out of the straw?" And when the stableboys came Stag was discovered and captured.

There is no eye like the master's.

THE YOUNG MAN AND THE SWALLOW

A FOOLISH MAN received his inheritance from his father, and lost no time in spending it in gambling and riotous living. The day the last of his fortune was lost he was walking along the road. It was wintertime, but the sun was shining and it was unseasonably warm. Foolish Swallow, pretending that it was spring, flew gaily around in the sky.

"It looks as though spring was here," said the foolish man. "I won't be needing all these clothes." So he pawned them, gambled with the proceeds, and lost.

But now, when he left the town, the sun was gone. Snow lay on the ground, and everything was frozen hard. Foolish Swallow, frozen stiff, lay dead in the snow. Looking at the dead bird, the shivering man said with chattering teeth: "It is all your fault that I am in this unhappy fix!"

There is no profit in blaming your foolish mistakes
on foolish advisers.

WOLF AND CRANE

THE WOLF once got a bone stuck in his throat. He had been greedy and eaten his meat too fast. The bone was sharp and gave him great pain. In vain he coughed and choked. The bone would not come out. He howled and screeched aloud.

"Help me, some creature!" he cried, as best he could. "Won't someone pull this bone out of my throat? Come along, Fox, you try."

But the fox refused. So did all the other animals. They hated Wolf, and no one was willing to help him.

"If someone doesn't help me, I shall die," moaned Wolf. "If anyone gets this bone out, I'll give him a handsome reward."

Now the crane, a tall bird with a long bill, happened to be passing and overheard the wolf's lament. He took pity on him and offered to help. Besides, the idea of a reward tempted him.

"I can do him a good turn, poor fellow," he thought, "and get something for myself into the bargain."

So Crane put his long bill down into Wolf's throat, seized the bone, and gave it a sharp tug. Wolf howled with pain, but the bone came out.

"There," said Crane, "that's it. Feeling better? What about my reward?"

"What reward?" snarled Wolf, showing his yellow teeth. "Why, you ungrateful bird! You've just put your head down the throat of a wolf without getting it bitten off. No other creature has done that! And that's your reward, you lucky bird! Fly away, before I gobble you up."

Crane didn't stop to argue, but did as he was told.

Those who help a rogue in hope of gain
mustn't grumble if their trouble goes unrewarded.

The Wolf and the Crane

The Wolf and the Lamb

As a wolf was lapping at the head of a running brook he spied a lamb daintily paddling her feet some distance down the stream.

"There's my supper," thought Wolf. "But I'll have to find some excuse for attacking such a harmless creature."

So he shouted down at Lamb: "How dare you stir up the water I am drinking and make it muddy?"

"But you must be mistaken," bleated Lamb. "How can I be spoiling your water, since it runs from you to me and not from me to you?"

"Don't argue," snapped Wolf. "I know you. You are the one who was saying those ugly things about me behind my back a year ago."

"Oh, sir," replied Lamb, trembling, "a year ago I was not even born."

"Well," snarled Wolf, "if it was not you, then it was your father, and that amounts to the same thing. Besides, I'm not going to have you argue me out of my supper."

Without another word he fell upon helpless Lamb and tore her to pieces.

Any excuse will serve a tyrant.

The Tortoise and the Eagle

THE TORTOISE ONCE upon a time was not the contented fellow that he is today. There was a time when he wished with all his heart that he could fly. As he watched the birds disporting themselves in the clouds he felt sure that if he could get up into the air he could soar with the best of them.

One day he called to Eagle who was hovering overhead: "Friend Eagle, you are the best flier among all the birds. If you will teach me to fly I will bring you all the treasures of the sea."

Eagle replied: "But you are asking the impossible, friend Tortoise. In the first place, you have no wings and, in the second, nature never intended you to fly."

But Tortoise kept pleading and promising greater and greater rewards. So finally Eagle said that he would do the best he could. Telling Tortoise to hang on, he bore him high into the sky. Then he loosed his hold upon Tortoise, now thoroughly frightened, and cried: "All right, start flying."

Poor Tortoise, however, dropped like a stone and was dashed to pieces on the rocks below.

Vanity carries its own punishment.

THE LION, THE DONKEY AND THE FOX

LION, A DONKEY, and a fox formed a hunting party, and after an exciting chase caught and killed a great stag. All three were hungry, but Lion especially so. "Here, friend Donkey," he roared, "divide up the spoils, and let's have our dinner. I'm just about starved."

Donkey was trying his best to divide the carcass into three equal portions when Lion fell upon him with a roar and tore him to pieces.

"Now," said Lion to Fox, "let's see how good you are at dividing the stag into two parts."

Taking one look at the remains of poor Donkey, Fox said never a word, but made sure that in the division of the meat he left the "lion's share" for the King of Beasts and only a mouthful for himself.

Lion nodded approvingly. "A very fair division, indeed," said he. "Who could have taught you to divide so fairly?"

"If I needed any lesson," replied Fox, "I had only to look at the body of our late friend, Donkey, over yonder."

We learn by the misfortunes of others.

THE HEN AND THE CAT

LL THE barnyard knew that Hen was indisposed. So one day Cat decided to pay her a visit of condolence. Creeping up to her nest Cat in his most sympathetic voice said: "How are you, my dear friend? I was so sorry to hear of your illness. Isn't there something that I can bring you to cheer you up and to help you feel like yourself again?"

"Thank you," said Hen. "Please be good enough to leave me in peace, and I have no fear but I shall soon be well."

Uninvited guests are often most welcome when they are gone.

THE WOLF AND THE SHEPHERDS

A WOLF chanced to be looking through the doorway of a hut where some shepherds were comfortably regaling themselves upon a joint of mutton. As he heard them smack their lips over the juicy morsels and watched them carving the roasted carcass with their knives, his lips curled with scorn.

Said he to himself: "These shepherds seem mightily pleased with themselves. But what would they do if they were to observe me partaking of a similar supper?"

Men are too apt to condemn in others the very things
they do themselves.

THE HEN AND THE FOX

FOX WAS out looking for a late supper. He came to a hen-house, and through the open door he could see a hen far up on the highest perch, safe out of reach.

Here, thought Fox, was a case for diplomacy. Either that or go hungry! So he gave considerable thought to just how he should approach his intended supper.

"Hello, there, friend Hen," said he in an anxious voice. "I haven't seen you about of late. Somebody told me that you have had a sick spell and I was sincerely worried about you. You look as pale as a ghost. If you will just step down I'll take your pulse and look at your tongue. I'm afraid you are in for quite a siege."

"You never said a truer word, cousin Fox," replied Hen. "It will have to be a siege, for I am in such a state that if I were to climb down to where you are, I'm afraid it would be the death of me."

Beware of the insincere friend!

THE EAGLE AND THE FOX

AN EAGLE and a fox long had lived together as good neighbours, Eagle at the top of a high tree and Fox in a hole at the foot of it. One day, however, while Fox was away, Eagle, seeking a tender morsel for her nestful of young ones, swooped down upon Fox's cub and carried it away to her nest.

Fox, on her return home, scolded Eagle for this breach of friendship, and pleaded with Eagle to return the cub to her den. But Eagle, feeling sure that her own brood high up in their treetop nest were safe from any possible revenge, ignored the entreaties of the cub's mother.

Quickly running to the place where she knew an altar fire to be burning, Fox snatched a brand and hurried back to the tree. Mother Eagle, who was just on the point of tearing the cub to pieces to feed to her babies, looked down and saw that Fox was going to set fire to the tree and burn it and her nest and eaglets to ashes.

"Hold on, dear neighbour!" she screamed. "Don't set fire to our tree. I'll bring back your cub to you safe and sound!"

Do unto others as you would have them do unto you.

THE MOUSE AND THE FROG

OR MOUSE, it was an evil day when he made the acquaintance of Frog on the eve of a journey into the country. Protesting his great affection, Frog persuaded Mouse to allow him to go along. But we shall never know what possessed Mouse when he let Frog tie one of his own forefeet to one of Frog's hindfeet, for surely it made travelling most uncomfortable indeed.

However, they limped and hopped along the path until they came to a stream of water. Frog immediately jumped in, saying: "Follow me, friend Mouse, and have no fear. You may find the harness a bit awkward, but remember that I'll be right by your side as we swim across."

So they began to swim. Scarcely had they reached midstream, however, when Frog took a sudden plunge to the bottom, dragging the unfortunate mouse after him. The struggling and threshing of Mouse caused such a great commotion in the water that it attracted the attention of a hawk sailing in the sky overhead. Swift as lightning he pounced down upon the drowning Mouse and carried him away. And with them, of course, went Frog as well.

He who compasses the destruction of his neighbour
is often caught in his own snare.

THE FOX AND THE BRAMBLE

HE HOUNDS WERE in full cry in pursuit of wily Fox and were gaining on him rapidly. Turning suddenly from his course, Fox dived through a hedge that was full of sharp thorns.

"Those dogs will never follow me through these brambles," said Fox to himself.

Just then he stepped on one of the thorns.

"That was a dirty trick," he snarled. "What kind of bramble are you? Here I come to you for help, but you only stab me for my pains."

"Wait a minute, friend Fox," replied Bramble. "I'm the one who should be angry. You came running to me for help with your tail between your legs. I didn't ask you to come this way, did I? You knew I had thorns, and you were perfectly willing to have the dogs wounded by them. Now that you, yourself, got caught on one of them you complain. Next time I hope the hounds catch you!"

All that Fox could do was lick his smarting paw.

To the selfish all are selfish.

THE MAN AND HIS TWO WIVES

A WHILE AGO, in the days when a man was allowed more wives than one, a middle-aged bachelor whose hair was only just beginning to turn grey fell in love with two women at one time, and married both of them.

One was young and blooming, and wished her husband to appear as youthful as herself. So every night she would comb his hair, and as she did so she would pull out all the grey hairs.

The other wife, who was older, saw her husband growing grey with pleasure, for she did not like to be mistaken for his mother. So each morning when she brushed his hair she would industriously pluck out every black hair she could find.

For a time the man enjoyed the attention and devotion of his wives, until one morning when he looked into the mirror and found that he was completely bald.

Yield to the caprices of all and you soon will have
nothing to yield at all.

THE MOUNTAIN IN LABOUR

THERE WAS A day when the people of a certain country heard a mighty rumbling in the near-by mountain. Smoke was pouring from the summit. The earth was trembling, and great rocks came hurtling down into the valley. The mountain seemed to be in labour, and all the people rushed to a vantage point where they could see what terrible thing was about to happen.

They waited and waited, while the sky grew dark and the rumblings and thunderings increased. Finally, as the people watched, there was one earthquake more violent than all the others. Suddenly, a huge fissure appeared in the side of the mountain. The people threw themselves down upon their knees. Some of them fainted. All the rest waited with bated breath to see what would happen next.

The thundering stopped. A deep silence fell. And out of the gap in the side of the mountain popped a mouse!

Magnificent promises often end in paltry performances.

THE QUACK FROG

A FROG, EMERGED from the mud of the swamp, announced to all the animal world that he could cure every manner of disease. Interested to see what all the croaking was about, the animals gathered around, and Frog, more puffed up than ever by the attention he was receiving, bellowed:

"Here, come and see! You are looking upon the greatest physician in all the world. Not even Aesculapius, Jove's court doctor—"

He was interrupted by a loud bray from Jackass. Goat, also, seemed to be somewhat sceptical of Frog's boastings and said so. Then up spoke Fox: "How dare you set up to heal others? Why do you not try first to cure your own limping gait?"

"And your own blotched and wrinkled skin," added Hare.

"And your own bulging and ugly eyes," said Sheep.

At this the Quack Frog drew in his head and hopped away in the direction of the bog from where he had come while the animals laughed him to scorn.

Physician, heal thyself!

THE THREE TRADESMEN

THE ENEMY stood outside the walls of a certain city. As they brought up their siege weapons and arranged their forces for the attack, the desperate defenders within held a council of war to determine the best means of holding their city.

A bricklayer arose. "Sirs," said he, "it is my opinion that the best material for this purpose is brick." Then he sat down.

A carpenter asked to be recognized. "I beg to differ with the bricklayer. The material that will best serve our desperate needs is wood. Let timber be our defence!"

Then a tanner jumped to his feet. "Citizens," he cried, "when you all have had your say, I wish to remind you that there is nothing in the world like leather!"

*It is difficult to see beyond
one's own nose.*

THE MONKEY AND THE DOLPHIN

HERE WAS an old custom among sailors to take with them on their voyages monkeys and other pets to amuse them while they were at sea. So it happened that on a certain voyage a sailor took with him a monkey as a companion on board ship.

Off the coast of Sunium, the famous promontory of Attica, the ship was caught in a violent storm and was wrecked. All on board were thrown into the water and had to swim for land as best they could. And among them was Monkey.

Dolphin saw him struggling in the waves, and taking him for a man, went to his assistance. As they were nearing the shore just opposite Pireaus, the harbour of Athens, Dolphin spoke. "Are you an Athenian?" he asked.

"Yes, indeed," replied Monkey, as he spat out a mouthful of sea water. "I belong to one of the first families of the city."

"Then, of course, you know Piraeus," said Dolphin.

"Oh, yes," said Monkey, who thought Piraeus must be the name of some distinguished citizen, "he is one of my very dearest friends."

Disgusted by so obvious a falsehood, Dolphin dived to the bottom of the sea and left Monkey to his fate.

Those who pretend to be what they are not,
sooner or later, find themselves in deep water.

THE SHEPHERD AND THE SEA

THE GRAZING being poor in the hills, a shepherd moved his flock down near the shore where the sea mist kept the grass fresh and green. As he guarded his sheep he delighted in gazing out over the tranquil sea, so smooth and calm and limitless. One day he was seized with a strong desire to sail over that peaceful expanse of blue water.

So the shepherd sold his flock and received a good price because of the fatness of the sheep. With the money he bought a cargo of dates which he loaded on a vessel and set sail for another port. He had not gone far, however, when the sky became dark and a storm arose. The boat was driven upon the rocks and wrecked, and his cargo of dates and everything he owned was swallowed up by the sea. Indeed, it was only by good fortune that the one-time shepherd was rescued and able to get to land.

Not long after this unhappy experience, the shepherd was sitting sorrowfully on the shore looking out to sea (which was now calm and serene once more) when one of his friends came up to him and said: "I see you are admiring the ocean. How beautiful and tranquil is the sea. Could any sight be more inviting!"

"Have a care, my good fellow," replied the shepherd sourly, "of that smooth surface; it is only looking out for your dates."

Trust not in him that seems a saint.

A Dog and a Butcher

S THE BUTCHER was busy about his meat, Dog ran away with a sheep's heart. The butcher saw him running away with a piece of flesh in his mouth, and called out after him, "Listen, friend, you may even make the best of your purchase, as long as you've made me wiser for it."

Those who learn through misfortune
lose nothing.